TWO

WEDDINGS

AND A

BUST

A

Novel

by

Genie Chow

ISBN 979-8-218-44640-6

Author, Illustration and Book Design by Genie Chow

Title: Two Weddings and a Bust/Genie Chow

Subjects: Romantic comedy, Love stories, Wit and
Humor

Dedication

To all my family and friends
who encouraged me to write.
Thank you all, you deserve the
best.

Chapter One

It was a bright new day, and the sun streamed through the windows at Penchant Productions film production studio. Annie Chen, the youthful-looking story editor's assistant checked the calendar on her monitor.

"Your ten o-clock appointment with Lou Stern is coming up, just as a reminder," said Annie, who looked ten years younger than her 46 years. She turned eagerly from her computer to Laura, co-producer of the finished film project, "Lovers in Venice".

"That's fine, Annie," she replied, "But tell him I'll be running about twenty minutes late. I've got to discuss the screenplay for our latest film shoot with Dan, and then I'll be able to give my full attention to Lou." Lou Stern was an executive producer at Penchant, with Laura and her husband, Dan Wood, as story editors at the studio. Annie quickly made note of that on a post-it note as she moved back to her monitor. Her energy and instincts were on high, and she was glad she had this job, overlooking a view of the sunny Los Angeles skyline, a far cry from her hometown of Mackinac Island in Michigan.

Her job was set in a polished office high-rise environment with a successful film studio in Hollywood. One that had success in the romantic comedy and romance drama genres. Her duties included the handling the screenplay revisions to send to directors, scouring the library of source material for ideas and handling screenplay submissions to the studio.

At home in her spare time she worked on her movie script, hoping when it was finished, to pitch it to just the right person. At 200 pages, it needed to be edited down to 98, if she wanted it to pass as a romantic comedy. She was overwhelmed with the work she had to do.

On break in the ladies room, she took a look at her face. The fine lines and puffiness around her eyes began to show signs of her hard work writing her script. Would she look better with plastic surgery? She smoothed out the sags with her fingers again.

Heaven forbid, you won't ever risk that, she said to herself. What other women did, not for me. I like to age gracefully, she thought. But as she debated about what it would be like to spend a fortune on a lifetime supply of Frownie tape to rid herself of facial wrinkles forever, she looked at the time.

Sighing over the work she was taking on; she took a measured sip from her cup of hot coffee. She thought back to when she got this position, after she accepted and completed an interning gig at the other rival film production company, Atlas Pictures.

Former rivals, that is.

The executive producers for both companies were in the planning stages of a partnership and merger, to make up a celebratory Nine Figure Pictures, as the smaller company, Atlas couldn't exist without Penchant taking over. Atlas Pictures was in a bind. Their finances were frozen due to money owed to creditors. It was due to the generosity of Lou and the other executive producers that the employees at Atlas and Penchant would be able to keep their positions while the merger was taking place, and afterwards, when everything was finalized.

Annie, ever capable and versatile, with her stylish black hair tousled and framing her face, had been with Penchant Productions since six months ago, when she graduated from a screenwriting bootcamp and started working on her first screenplay. It was something she hoped would lead to a movie deal within the company, after the merge was complete. Grabbing a sip of her coffee, she paused, more alert and focused, as she smiled to herself. This was the perfect position for her. Life was great, she had a beautiful relationship with her parents, her sister, this job … hold on, I better get back to work, stop daydreaming now, she reminded herself.

Everything was going great for Annie, except for one thing. It was the guys she had been meeting. She wasn't doing very well in the relationship department, as she described it. Last year when she accepted a position as a story editing assistant at Atlas Pictures, she started dating Bill. Bill the Bachelor, as he was nicknamed. Bill would go around selling his services as an ad manager within Atlas and Penchant, selling more than his promotional materials.

Even some of the older, more experienced female staff fell victim to his intimidations. Annie was one of those women who fell for him, just because she was tired of feeling lonely. He was around her age, but she was really looking for a long-term relationship, and Bill was a playboy, turning women's heads with his dark locks and sometimes pleasant manner.

But there was something shady in his actions. He was younger than most of his dates and he brought out the cougar in any unwitting older, but goodie, women in the offices at the two movie production companies. I like this position better, she thought to herself. She really liked Laura and Dan.

The dating game had been just that, a game for Annie. She was afraid of commitment. Even she said she was trying to fix that aspect of her life. She told herself she was a serial monogamist, seeking change. Or she was giving herself the excuse that she didn't have time for a real relationship. Plain and simple. She would have one-night stands, four-night flings, dating for a month or two, then breakups, you name it. And doubting her own potential, she would be crestfallen whenever a friend or relative were planning their wedding and blissfully walking down the aisle.

In a few months she would turn 47. She couldn't even get past the first date sometimes. It wasn't like she was unattractive. She was just tired of meeting men who only wanted one thing, to be her sex partner. Annie had a sweet face and temperament, and she had a youthful, slender body to match. Except for a little paunch in her stomach. Better work on that one, she thought.

Bill had met Annie after securing a deal with the media department to distribute Atlas Pictures' romance drama "Finding Her", currently streaming on video. "Let's meet for dinner," he said, almost commanding her. "We have a lot of business to take care of."

After a quiet dinner at an Italian restaurant, where the food was the best in that part of L.A., she decided it would be alright to go to his place and find out more about him. Once they got inside after he poured her some red wine, she took a few sips. Bill had cornered her in his house's dark hallway and forced a kiss on her. The two hadn't been intimate with anyone for awhile, and both were hungry for attention. But since it was more like a one-night stand based on passion rather than friendship, the relationship quickly fizzled over and she felt lost, confused and used when she didn't hear back from him. Snap back to the present. Just at that moment in the office, the phone rang.

"Hi, Bill?" she said, glancing at the caller ID. As if she was expecting something. She had her instincts on high again. She wanted to feel accepted by him, not knowing why.

"Honestly, we're not a good match. But I enjoy our sex," he said, woodenly. "So if you want to continue as an in-between relationship, I'm all for it. I would rather go to a friend than see a prostitute. I could see a prostitute, but I would rather see a *friend*. It just makes it convenient for me." As if trying to make a sales deal with her, his words left a sickening feeling in her gut.

Annie fumed inside. She couldn't believe what she was hearing. Filled with anger and embarrassment, she wondered what she had gotten into that made this happen to her. I'm not a prostitute! She thought to herself, struggling to contain her feelings as she hastily hung up the phone. And I was not acting like a prostitute with him, a voice in her defended herself. If only…

"Annie, can you call the party store and the caterers to plan our wrap party?" Laura appeared again at Annie's office door. An energetic woman in her fifties, she wore a close-fitting jersey dress and tights and had a youthful charm about her. "It's going to be great. And of course, we'd love it if you could make it."

Annie had been looking forward to this for the past couple of days after the production company prepared to celebrate the work done on their current film project. "No problem, I'd love that!" she smiled, suddenly perky, her eyes sparkling with a grin on her face that instantly lit up a room, even behind her cat-eye eyeglasses. If it wasn't for this job she adored, she didn't know where she would be. More daydreaming to herself.

She would have to schedule a daytime delivery with Allie, Laura and Dan's daughter. "Allie, it's nice to see you. I heard you're volunteering as a production assistant today?" She glanced at one of the black steampunk lace dresses Allie wore every day.

"Where do these go," Allie asked, unassumingly pulling on the ribbons tied to some stray balloons. She lowered her eyes, rimmed with heavy kohl black eyeliner. Annie pointed to an array of bright mylar balloons. She wanted her to open up a little more, as she seemed kind of shy. Kind of like she was when she was a teenager. "Just put those in the spare room," Annie said, gesturing to a room in the back. Maybe I was ordering her around too much, thought Annie, as Allie sighed and pushed the balloons to the back.

"I know what you can do, she smiled, warmly, to the young woman. "You can write down a list for the caterers at the staff party," as she opened the door to the supply closet outside of her office and pulled out a marker and paper pad for Allie, who was twirling her hair on the side of her face, with the rest of her hairdo in a high, messy bun.

"Some croissants would be nice," she said, her face more relaxed. "Excellent idea," Annie smiled. "And fresh finger foods, like broccoli, grape tomatoes, dip, and six bottles of Merlot...", she counted on her fingers, pausing as Allie began making notes. "Can you think of anything else?"

"Yeah, fresh fruit bowls would be great!" Her face perked up.

"Good job! You can just put the list over there, and I can make some calls."

12 noon. She would take care of the party arrangements requests that afternoon. There was much work to do and Annie was looking forward to it. After making another refreshing cup of vanilla flavored joe for herself, she sat in the adjoining dining area and settled into her lunch, savoring the slightly sweet croissant turkey sandwich she had bought at the bakery a short drive from the production company.

She got a ring on her phone. "Annie, can you come in for a moment?" It was Laura, her voice insistent. "Annie, I wanted to discuss this with you," as Annie took a seat in Laura's office. After a pause, she said, "I'll be moving on to another position within the company in August, as an assistant director before I retire. I thought, who would be best for the position I'm leaving as story editor? You have the qualities I'm looking for to fill this position. Is this something you would like to consider?"

Annie fidgeted in her seat a bit, then replied after a few moments. "That seems like a good choice for me," she said, thoughtfully. I've got so much on my plate now, should I tell her how I feel?

Instead, she looked straight at Laura, and said, "I think I can handle that," but her mind wandered back to her writing. How will I have time for that, too? she asked herself. But the story editor position was a step up from an assistant. How could anyone in her shoes refuse? "Yes, I would like to take that on," she said, as enthusiastically as she could sound.

"Good!" So we'll start the transition in August. Alright with you?"

"Yes!" She smiled, putting on her Miss Goody Two Shoes face. She couldn't afford to say no. She didn't want to risk losing her job. Or disappointing Laura.

It wasn't too busy today, so she had time to talk to her friend Gayle, the script supervisor signed on for the latest production. Annie worked closely with her, bringing copies of revisions on screenplays to her so she could keep up with the changes and make sure the actors' lines were on point, or didn't stray too much from ad-libbing.

A friend of Annie's since she first started work there, Gayle was an attractive dark-haired woman in her sixties. She wore her hair in a topknot that gave her an air of sophistication. Annie hadn't talked about Bill to anyone but her, after she first started dating him.

"How has it been dating Bill? I know he has a reputation," she asked, as Annie replied quickly, "It hasn't been. I'm not seeing him anymore," her eyes a bit wet. But she tried hard to hold back the tears. Annie didn't expect anybody to care about her.

"Are you alright, Annie?" She looked at her friend, closely. Annie's eyes moistened again as she wiped her tears and nose with a tissue. Gayle smiled, knowingly. "You know, it's probably best it happened that way. Maybe you should just concentrate on work. You seem to enjoy it a lot, and," she looked straight at Annie, "who knows, this could lead to something even better for you when you least expect it." A strong voice inside Annie said to herself, "I can do this. I can get control over myself."

Gayle even confided, "Annie, I'm going through a period where the man I'm seeing wants to take time off from our relationship." She sighed. Everybody knew she was dating Charles, the line producer for the upcoming production, "He's All Mine", the first of the merger Nine Figure Pictures. It seemed she was holding it in for awhile, too.

She focused on Gayle, her brows furrowed, listening intently. "It's been hard, he used to bring me flowers every day for weeks when we first met. But we were spending a lot of time together and not paying attention to work." She looked away, saying, "Things took a bad turn where we would argue every night. So I'm on a hiatus from him. We're just keeping it professional now." She crossed her arms, saying, "I am hoping things will work out. I can't stand the thought of him dating someone else, but who knows, it may be best that way," she said.

"Gayle, if there's anything I can do to help, or just listen to you, I will do that," said Annie, putting her hand on her friend's shoulder.

It was this realization that made it clear to Annie how unsafe she had been with Bill, getting so intimate with him at the drop of a hat. She wasn't alone. Even couples who were friends first had their problems, but she knew this was even more of a dilemma with Bill. She had brief relationships with others before, but since she was looking for something long term, it hurt her badly. She hadn't even seen him for awhile, or contacted him much, except for a few back and forth emails and a phone call. She felt he was being abrupt and obnoxious, and hesitated to go out with him.

And he body shamed her. "You've got skinny legs. Like a giraffe. And you have this whiny voice, your stomach's not flat …" while he was dating her, and of course Annie wanted out of the relationship. In a last-minute effort to save the relationship, he said to her, "Maybe you can look up some sex positions while at work and we can try them out." All of which Annie did not feel was appealing, in all the least.

She wanted more out of a relationship, from someone who cared.

Annie tried to pull herself away from the image of her going to Bill's place with a bucket of water and splashing it over him to cool him down, he needed it so badly. Nope. Didn't want to even bother with that. This is something not crying for. I'm not going to stand for it, she thought to herself, firmly.

She determined, staunchly, as she brushed the hair from her face and sent off party invitations online, that she wouldn't settle for less anymore.

Chapter Two

Annie walked over to the nearest and favorite coffee shop of the Penchant crew, Cuppa Joe, adjacent to the production company's parking lot. She took out a pen and notepad she always kept in her purse for those unexpected ideas bubbling around in her head. She overheard a young couple sitting in a well-worn love seat, draping arm and arm together as they sipped their café lattes. She overheard their giggles and later, snuck a look at their intimate kisses that they weren't very self-conscious in giving to each other. They recounted the escapades of their classmates.

"That girl in our class, she's always studying and never talks to anyone. I don't want to be anything like her," the female college student remarked, a bit arrogantly.

Ohhh, look at you …. do you think you're better?" he smiled, laughing and squeezing her shoulder arm.

"Nooo," she playfully punched his arm. "I just don't want to end up a bookworm like her when I start my classes."

"What are you getting so snobby about? I thought you were looking forward to your classes in social studies? Isn't that the study of people?"

"Yeah, but I like to hang out with my friends once in awhile. Like you," she rubbed noses with him. "Oh my god, get a room," thought Annie, but she was taking notes.

"Just remember, we meet your mom and dad next week," the young guy looked deep into her eyes.

The young woman crossed her arms, defensively. "Oh yeah, I forgot. You better not start an argument with me in front of them. You did that last time we saw *your* parents …"

She playfully punched him in the arms several times again. "OK now you're getting on my nerves," he punched back.

"Hey, stop that," she giggled. "Stop!" more seriously this time. "I'm not going to meet with them if you don't stop!"

Annie looked over her shoulder at them again and sighed, taking more notes.

"OK, OK, I was only kidding," the guy stopped and replaced it with a hug. Now get a room, Annie thought to herself, and she took off in her car, in a writing mood.

Fumbling with her keys, without hesitating, she crossed through the doorway, went to the kitchen in her apartment and made herself a noontime fruit smoothie with spinach and protein powder. Settling down in front of her computer, she continued working on her screenplay.

> KATE(over the phone)
> You know, it would have been nice if you told me about this after hours instead of calling me at work.

> JOSH(on the line)
> You're always nagging me. I wish you would stop.

> KATE
> I'm only saying this.
> I want our relationship to work.
> (pause)
> Weren't we going to meet with my parents? Like you said and keep saying?

> JOSH
> I still want to do that.
> But after I finish my exams.

The warm summer evening at Laura and Dan's house in Santa Monica welcomed buzzing cicadas in the rose bushes, and mostly welcomed members of the production team, even some crew members and miscellaneous referrals, who were friends of Laura and Dan's for the past six years. Laura was well-respected by her employees, who appreciated her positive attitude and attention to their needs.

She smiled and greeted Annie, who arrived early to make a last-minute call to the caterers and remind them about the party. "Hello, Annie, glad you could make it," she beamed. "I didn't want to miss out," Annie smiled back. "On all the fun." Life wasn't as fun as she hoped in her personal life, but she really wanted to be here.

"Hello, Charles!" Laura greeted the line producer, a burly man with a youthful attitude who didn't mind working a little beyond his usual set of hours. "Yes, Laura. It's been a hectic week. I'm still trying to keep our budget afloat and get our editors to finish in time by next week. So, technically, it isn't over yet. I keep telling Brad, our assistant director, he has to let crew members know there are new shots we need to have done, and at the same location next time. It will still keep our movie within the budget."

"Charlie, we really appreciate the work you do. Would you say in a few weeks our movie will be all set for distribution?" He nodded, then lifted his arms to hug her. "A reason to celebrate!" She drew her arms around him and returned a hug, then focused her attention on Annie again.

"We'll have some friends in our screenwriting department we've invited that you may want to meet."

"That would be great," Annie smiled. But not so great. She began to sweat, anxiously. She shifted her weight from one foot to the other, not wanting to tell Laura her screenplay was still in the revision stage, as it might stall their interest in her project. But

21

maybe she could at least introduce herself.

"I've got to get it past the rough draft stage, though," she said. "Anyone in the production could be a valuable contact, but if you're not ready I won't let them know," Laura said. Annie thought she may be overeager, but the idea that she may be able to get them to read over the first five pages of her screenplay popped into her mind. Not now, thought Annie. She even thought of approaching Laura and Dan, but she wanted to avoid a conflict of interest.

The night was invigorated with the sound of an old record of jazz music. Dan's goal of creating a relaxing, supportive atmosphere was coming to life. Smiling, and taking in the mellow sounds, Annie cheered up and boosted her confidence level.

"And this new film, I heard is already getting the attention of our marketing pros," she said to Gretchen, a European woman in a sequined black blouse, the film's main costume designer."

"Oh, yes," she said in a heavy accent, "Charles made sure of that. He's been named a director of considerable talent." Including them, they made up a crowd of about forty-five participants, some dressed casually, others in more formal dress in subdued colors. The room was buzzing with the laughter of hardworking professionals taking it easy for a change for a well-deserved break from the rigors of their craft.

Finally, the caterers arrived, greeting their hosts with informal hellos. The talk was about how well the company was doing this summer, how their kids were doing and what some of the older ones' plans were for going back to college, some part-timers, some full-time employees, some following their footsteps in the movie business.

It was all interesting, but Annie couldn't stop comparing herself inside of her thoughts. They're all just getting ahead of me, and I feel so left behind…..wonder what it would have been like if I had kids. But no, she was too busy with her career and time spent with her friends and family.

That didn't mean she didn't want time spent with someone special, for her. "And when are you going to tie the knot, Annie?" one of the story department staff asked. Annie fidgeted, shifting herself from one foot to another. She snapped back to the present.

"Well, I have to find the guy, first," to which a few laughed, except the one who asked her the question. Annie tried to keep her mind on the party, not her personal life. She knew they were trying to set her up with Jim, a would-be screenwriting student. She wasn't too passionate about him.

As a relief from this awkward moment, the caterers arrived with the appetizers, and later, an order from Dragon Inn Chinese restaurant she called about earlier. The room was filled with smells of barbecue pork and vegetarian mushu.

"O.K., everyone, we have our lovely dinner I ordered from the best Chinese restaurant in L.A," she announced, keeping her mind on the guests.

Annie was just done showing the caterers where to put the food in their warming trays, when she narrowed her vision and directed it towards a younger-looking man who was talking to the others they invited for dinner.

He seemed to be the center of attention with some of the guests and she focused in on him as if no one else was around. His light blonde hair that framed his handsome face was cleanly cut, and his build was stocky and solid. He dressed simply and informally, in a black T-shirt and jeans.

Kind of cute, she thought, even charming. Annie smiled at him, wearing a black skirt and a top with large green flowers. I should talk to him, she mused. Later that night, after the other guests had gone home, she went up to him.

With complete confidence and amazingly relaxed, considering all the pressure she had built up at work, plus her soon-to-be breakup, she opened up to him. "I'm Annie. What's your name?" she smiled.

"Ian. Ian McDrew," he replied, a bit taken aback by her assertiveness.

She smiled widely, a bit coyly. "I'm an artist and a screenwriter. I work at Penchant Productions."

"A screenwriter?" They both smiled at each other, and Annie asked, "Where do you work?"

"At a law office. I'm a law clerk at Bridges & Palmer. I'm from Huntington Beach. They stationed me here in L.A. for this assignment with Penchant Productions and Atlas Pictures. I know you're merging with Atlas Pictures to make up Nine Figure Films.

Looking straight in each other's eyes, Ian continued. "I mean, they may be selling out." He paused, trying to stay business-like. He was failing at that, but he tried. "I help handle the legal issues for this case, so I thought I'd get in touch with Laura and Dan here. It might be the best thing they do, I keep telling myself. For financial and artistic reasons."

After he asked and found out Annie was working in the story department, he shared his goals with her. It was easygoing speaking with him. And she felt naturally drawn to him, becoming more relaxed than she had ever felt in two years. "I'd like to pass the bar, and become a lawyer in the entertainment business. Right now I work with all different clients. This was an unusual case for us, working with Penchant Productions."

She liked his straightforwardness immediately.

Just to be sure, she asked his age. "I'm 39," he replied. "You're seven years younger than me. I'm 46. I'm old!" She immediately embarassed herself by saying that, especially the last part. She wasn't one to say she was getting older. Just aging, 46 joyfully going on 27 was more accurate. "You're not old!" he said, defending her. She liked the fact that he didn't seem to mind her age. Friends told her she looked ten years younger, that is, if you didn't notice her tiny potbelly. She exercised and most of the time didn't overeat.

"What kind of food do you like?" Another probing question. "I usually like meat and veggies, like a stew or casserole. "I like to eat vegetarian once in awhile."

"Really?" she felt the attraction, and she was drawn to him. "I like that too. Give the animals a break sometimes," she laughed, nervously.

"You know, you're pretty assertive. I mean, most women I know would wait to have the man go after them, but you're different." She took his comment for good, as a compliment. "Thank you," she told him. "I guess it paid off to read those chapters in the Assertive Woman," she giggled. Despite her breaking out into a sweat.

She smiled again. "I'd love to talk to you more. Here's my card," she said. Annie wasn't always bold, but she knew what she wanted. He felt a strong attraction to her, a strong innocence about her, and admired that she was so direct and confident in her approach. Annie was also delighted by him, friendly and willing to answer her questions, as ordinary and even scrutinizing as they may have been. And she thought he was handsome. Something about him really made Annie feel reassured and peaceful.

"OK everybody! Group photo!" cried Lisa from the editing department, as she shifted her long hair out of the way. Standing near the top of the ladder, she steadied her hands on her camera. "We're sending this to everyone here with Atlas Pictures and the others back at the office. This is a celebration of our union with them and we want to make a good impression for all involved." She began waving for the others to pose closer together so she could make sure everyone was in the photos.

At this, Annie's cell phone rang. "Hello?" she said, surprised.

"Yeah, is this Annie?" a monotone voice asked. It was Bill,

who was not in a good mood. "I'm outside. Please don't keep me waiting," he said, his voice insistent and odious.

Boldly, she answered back. "We're finishing up our wrap party, and taking a group photo, I can't talk to you," she said, and hung up. And for the last time. Nice excuse, she said to herself. She put him out of her mind and grinned with all the others.

This was supposed to be a time of celebration, and she was not going to let anyone ruin it for her.

Chapter Three

                        KATE
            Remember when we first
            met? I was so attracted to
            you when I saw you.

Josh makes a funny face and dances
unexpectedly, twisting his hips.

Kate laughs. And goes over to hug him.

                        JOSH
              You mean like this?

He continues being silly, wiggling his butt.

                        KATE (amused)
                Josh!

She moves over to give Josh a kiss.

                        KATE
                Muahh!

Annie took a break from her writing to spend a little time organizing her living space. She cleaned her whole place, OK, maybe not the windowsills, that would have to wait 'til next time, and her gaze fell on an upright stack of old National Geographic magazines. Sheflipped through them, saved at her place from a decade ago. They were given to her when her dad had moved from the family home to the neighboring condominium.

"Here, you can have these, Annie. Maybe you can use them. For reference to do your art. And you can read these articles." She had flipped through them and found some useful photos as inspirations for her painting, while reading some of the articles about people around the world.

Now she had skimmed through all of them, and they were just gathering dust and mildew on her bookshelf. This organizing was part of reducing her clutter, an assignment from her therapist to reduce clutter for people who hoard. She saw no reason to keep them now. Except for one of the issues which featured Michelle Yeoh, when she was younger, doing a daredevil stunt high up above at a location in Hong Kong with only a decorative rope to hold onto. That was a keeper.

These were the main things she hoarded, besides all that clothing she accumulated with her mailorder obsessions. And that shoe collection. She had almost every type of high heeled shoe in her closet. Some she put away to give away, some she kept just in case for a dressy event, even though she knew they were bad for her to wear. Just trying to be like a movie star, she thought, and would come back to earth after her foot ached from being crammed in those tight shoes. Ouch. Something she had to let her therapist know about. About her nasty shopping compulsions.

Her mind drifted to the screenplay bootcamp class she took. One of her classmates was Jim, a tall, seemingly nice man. He was all too happy to talk to her after class. He seemed pretty harmless. There was an eagerness and honesty in his manner that she was attracted to. He wasn't too physically attractive to her but she felt she could talk to him. Like a friend. Later, however, she found him really annoying. Furthermore, he said things that made her feel unsafe.

"My last girlfriend was in a car accident. I was driving and our other friend died in the crash."

"That must have been terrible for you!" She shuddered at the thought. It just didn't seem real.

When they walked out to the parking lot behind the studio, she looked at the condition of his car. Annie never thought of herself as a snob, but the broken-down state of his thirty-year old car turned her off. He had stuck a picture of a Hindu god onto his dashboard, for reasons she didn't know of yet, except when he told her later he was a practitioner of Zen Buddhism, although the two were different religions. Well, maybe he's reliable after all, and it doesn't hurt to make friends with a guy. A platonic friendship, she thought.

The next night, Jim invited her to his friends' house. Annie thought of Ian. She wanted to get to know him. Probably a better match than Jim, she thought. She wasn't sure about Jim. Even through the annoyances, though, he seemed like a nice guy. "Oh, yeah, I'm getting together to see Peter and Magnolia. They're friends of mine. You'll like them, I'm sure."

But Jim was kind of desperate. Really desperate. He told her about what his mom thought of their friendship. "Oh, yeah I just called her about it. She's fine. She's fine. She's just happy I have a girlfriend." Annie didn't feel like she was his girlfriend.

A waft of smoke circled the room they were in. The telltale smell of marijuana made the room stank. She was in the same place she was in high school, the rebel students throwing pot parties. She thought she was beyond that stage. Yet there she was, with Jim, with his pot-smoking friend Peter and his wife, Magnolia. She was from Germany and spoke with a thick accent. She wasn't exactly very friendly with Annie, which puzzled her until she realized Magnolia saw her as competition for attention.

Walking through the apartment after using their bathroom, she discovered rooms full of knockoff ladies designer jeans piled up in the bedroom on draped sheets, nightstands, everywhere. Clothes and unfolded fabric draped all over. "How weird….and creepy…." she felt inside. Well, I have a problem, too, but this is outrageous, she made a mental note to herself. Jim explained that Magnolia was having a hard time selling those designer jeans in their apartment and not in too good of a mood. And that Peter was thinking of divorcing her because of her unruly attitude and bad temper.

"You can use my laptop," said Jim, enthusiastically, I use it for work all the time." Annie thought he was sweet about this. A little strange sometimes, but a sweet guy.

"Oh good. I might want to order some clothes." Uh ohh, online shopping again. Excessive online shopping. She began shopping for clothes as they spoke. At this, her cell phone rang.

"Hello?" she said, nervously. Excited, she recognized the voice.

"Hi, is this Annie?" Annie was surprised at this. And felt it was her ticket out of this situation. Thankful he called, she replied, trying hard to be discreet.

"Hi Ian, I'm at Jim's place now. This guy I met at my bootcamp class."

"Here's my number," he responded, quickly. "Call me back later." She jotted down his number on the clothing catalogue she had brought with her. And told Jim she had to cancel the order for clothes because she couldn't afford it. And she really couldn't.

As if to cover up her disappointment in not buying more clothing, and her excitement over Ian, she remarked to Jim, pasting a smile on her face, "I love these shoes you gave me!" She looked down at the electric blue high-heeled pumps she wore, as she sat, sprawled on her side.

"Yeah, they look really good on you!" replied Jim. Even though she could hardly walk in them. She must have been making herself too comfortable in someone else's apartment, because Magnolia quietly and suddenly brought out a box of takeout pizza and put it on the floor. They started to eat, including Annie. Then Magnolia laid in on her. She didn't expect this at all.

"How dare you talk to someone else. You are supposed to be with Jim, your date, my friend!" Annie was too stunned to look at her face or even try to make sense of her face, which just seemed like a blur with curly red hair. Magnolia worked herself up in a fury.

"You people really make me angry. Don't you see how nice Jim is to take you out, and you have to talk to someone on the phone?!"

She stomped off with Jim to the other room. In a minute, there were noises of their laughter coming from the bedroom. Annie was curious about what was going on, but decided it wasn't any of her business. There must have been something going on between them because it looked like Jim was wiping his face of lipstick stains when he came back out of Magnolia and Peter's bedroom.

Annie was stunned as she looked at Jim's laptop again, while Peter stared at the television set. Probably stoned on pot, thought Annie. She could smell it. Japanese cartoons played on the T.V. Not a word from Peter. It was an awkward night. After that episode, it sobered Annie up quickly.

Finally, to Annie's relief, Jim and Annie left the apartment. When they were safely out of earshot, she went over the evening's small but significant events. At least to Annie they were. She was learning more about Jim and what dating him would be like. "Your friend Magnolia got really mad at me!"

"Oh, she's like that. Peter was talking about getting a divorce from her. And he smokes pot all the time." Matter-of-factly. As if he didn't ever think they were the wrong crowd for him. They walked towards the elevator in the aging apartment complex and pushed the button as it opened. The door slid along with a deep, low rumble.

Jim gave her a weird look, and smiled.

"I always imagine a dead person is going to be in there." She made a disgruntled face as Jim smirked. She was not amused. She just wanted to go home and sort through her clothing again, then work on a painting and write on her desktop.

Chapter Four

I'd love to see Kay sometime, she thought. As soon as she arrived home, she picked up her cell. Her sister might be interested in talking to her about what was going on in her life, and she hadn't seen her since last Christmas. Kay managed to persuade her to stop by for a birthday lunch at her house.

"Happy birthday, Annie," said Kay, a bright expression on her face, opening the front door to her house with a stucco interior. Kay's long salt and pepper hair fell naturally along her back, and she wore comfortable shoes that were recycled from plastic. Annie began talking even as she walked in, eager as she was to relate to her older sis by four years. "It was really terrible," she began, following Kay inside. "This guy, Jim? I thought he was nice at first but then he turned out to be creepy and not at all anyone I'd want to date."

Listening, Kay went inside the kitchen and opened the fridge. "Want some lemonade? The lemons are fresh from our garden, and they taste really sweet," she said.

Taking the glass, Annie continued. "I don't know. Maybe for a friendship. At least he's better for me than Bill the Bachelor." Kay poured herself a glass, sat down at the table and leaned on one elbow, thinking it over.

"This guy, Bill," Annie continued. "I had to break up with him, or should I say, more accurately, dump him, because he was getting insulting, really disparaging me. And he dated a lot of women who work at the two production companies. I'm just tired of casual dating."

Kay went back into the kitchen and brought out plates of takeout chicken, bok choy and noodles. "Kay, you shouldn't have! This is such a nice birthday lunch," she smiled. Annie must have been persuasive enough for Kay to keep listening, because she asked, "Who's Bill the Bachelor?" She took a bite of the Asian stir fry noodles she ordered from a nearby restaurant in Santa Monica.

"Oh, that's the guy who can't keep his hands to himself. The skirt chaser at work. He's dated a large number of women working at Penchant Productions and Atlas Pictures," even though Annie knew that "a large number" was more akin to almost all of the ladies of eligible age, although it could have included some young adult women/borderline teenagers. She didn't want to shock or worry her sis about the details. "I don't even think he'll be rehired after the merger. It would be hell to see him when we become Nine Figure Pictures."

Kay slurped down her noodles. She was silent for awhile. "So you definitely don't want to date *him* again." Kay wasn't one to open up about her own personal life. But she cared about Annie and felt fine about her husband, Kenneth.

She wanted to be a role model for her younger sister. "See, with Kenneth, he broke up with his first girlfriend *way* before he met me. It was a clean slate. I mean, *ideally*, don't you think you better wait for a relationship like that? Kenneth and I have worked out our differences, too. We had to have therapy sessions ..."

Annie cut her off at that. She shook her head. "I don't want to wait that long. I think for me, I'm already 47, and I'm actively looking now. I'm alright about it."

Kay cut through this. "Annie, you can figure it out. I've seen you do this hundreds of times. You don't have to share the details of your love life," she said, in between sips of the refreshing drink. "Wouldn't you rather talk about something else today? I mean, it *is* your birthday, after all.

"Why not? thought Annie, but she replied, "Alright, I get it." She thought maybe she had been reading too many Jane Austen books where the sisters dished out their true life romance stories. It might give herself a chance to relax and overcome her anxiety. But she didn't want to spoil the mood.

"Happy birthday," said Kay again, in all sincerity. "Thanks!" Annie felt more cheerful. Silently, Kay went back into the kitchen, and discreetly lit eleven candles on a small cake. Annie took a breath in, saying, "Kay! This is really a surprise, I wasn't expecting this. You didn't have to…"

The eleven candles were four plus seven, her age. Enjoying the sweetness of the carrot cake and cream cheese frosting, Annie kept rambling on about her futility in finding a mate. She couldn't keep it inside.

Kay went to the living room and picked up a tiny gift, wrapped in an exquisitely constructed box that was handmade in the colors of silver and lavender natural paper by Kay. "You didn't have to," Annie smiled, voice lowered. Inside was a tiny copper heart shaped box with the word Sister engraved on top. She opened it and there was a tiny light amethyst heart-shaped stone inside, her birthstone.

"Kay, thank you. This is really nice…" Kay smiled back, wearily. Maybe it was because Kay was bored over Annie talking about her love life, so she told her, "Hey, Annie? Can we talk more another time? I have to pick up Jill from school now. And Leeland can't miss his wrestling class." Again she couldn't even think about what her life would be like with her own children, she mused. It would mean so much time away from her writing and art.

"Some people can juggle things, work, play, having kids … like *you*, Kay. I love children but they're not for me," Annie reminded herself and Kay, too. She did want children before, but she was past that age. In a way she accepted that. She needed more time for herself. And there was nothing wrong with that.

Chapter Five

                    KATE
          Am I thinking too hard?
          We're going to need
          some me time. Some time
          just doing what we want
          to do on our own, instead
          of arguing.

                    JOSH
          Some things don't need to
          be said.

                    KATE
          OK. I trust us.
          (suddenly changing her mood)
            Remember when we had lunch
            together for the first
            time? We really did have
            fun.

In the next month or so, over the phone, she convinced herself she

couldn't be hurt by dating Jim. It's all harmless, she mused. More like platonic, she reminded herself again. She mostly connected to him by phone. And she actually admitted to herself it was fun chatting with him, until he said something that really bothered her, in his very annoying, happy-go-lucky voice. He kept pressuring her. "Hey, I wonder if when you do your sales pitch for your screenplays, if you wore a tight sexy dress and makeup, maybe you could sell your screenplays better that way. You know, like you could flirt with them …"

He even bought a screenplay pitch book that he promised to let her read, but he never did. And he never did start writing a screenplay of his own. She felt like laughing about this, but she had never experienced someone like this before. This was particularly irksome for her.

And how he boasted more times than once that he was such a good salsa dancer Mexican people were shocked that he was a white guy able to dance so well. Her only sin was she carried on with him even when she knew she didn't like him much. She even persuaded him to shop at the discount clothing store with her when they were in her neighborhood. That was where she convinced him to buy those overstock pair of electric blue stiletto pumps for her.

She checked her voicemail. Ian had left a message. "Hi Annie. Did you want to get together? Alright, call me back."

"Hi Ian, "It's Annie, I got your message. Annie called back, without a moment's hesitation,

"Do you wanna listen to some live music tomorrow night?

There's a really great jazz club in downtown LA."

"OK, I'll do that with you," he replied. No nonsense or idle chatter taking up precious time. Just straight talk from someone she was beginning to like even more.

"Meet me at the Hollywood and Vine Metro stop. At five o'clock," she said. She never felt more eager. Spritzing on some Juicy Couture perfume, one of the knockoff ones at sale prices from the drugstore, she sneezed and rubbed her nose. I guess I'm no better than Jim, she ruminated. He always wore this stinky men's cologne that turned her off just thinking about it. It was about an hour later when she arrived downtown and left the train station to wait for Ian.

Just outside of the station, bustling with passengers who couldn't wait to go home, she walked along and answered her cell phone. Spotting Ian waiting at the station, across the street, standing firmly and decisively, he said, "Hey, I'm here. Where are you?" he asked, a little confused, getting lost in the ever-rising sound of people on the street.

A large crowd formed into an impromptu parade, but she didn't notice anything different until later, being so focused on meeting Ian. Even more people gathered from the crowd and walked along Hollywood Boulevard, oblivious to the Walk of Fame stars on the sidewalk. Most were ten years younger than them, in their twenties and thirties. She asked a young woman in cutoff jeans and Sherpa boots what was going on.

"It's the LovElectronic Music Festival," she replied, facing forward, not too eager to be explaining things, engrossed in the crowd wearing all sorts of hippie garb and seventies outfits, some with tambourines shaking to the electronic music.

A horn section playing over DJ Flacks and electro pop music led the floats in the parade.

Annie looked at Ian again in front of the station as she called out on her cell phone. "Ian! I'm coming to meet you...I see you. Don't move!" she raised her voice, trying to be heard above the music. More music fans started to shimmy to the sounds, some break dancing in sixties outfits, ladies in bras and panties, the infectious dance music rising louder around the two, as they got lost in the whirl of the crowd. When they finally found each other, Ian was agitated.

"Let's get out of here! I wanna lose this crowd!" he shouted over the din. "I didn't know they were having this festival. Someone told me it's the LovElectronic Music Festival," she explained, as the whole street was taken up by even more party people in colorful clothes.

She linked her arm in his arm so they wouldn't lose each other, as bands of revelers, more people with multicolored hair in skimpy, skin-baring costumes, filled the streets. There were young women in tie-dyed bikini tops and young, bare-chested guys in striped, baggy pants. It was almost entertaining on its own, just watching them.

Shouting so Ian could hear, "Oh yeah, I remember now! This festival was started in San Francisco! And it got so popular they have one here, too!" She fought to be heard above the pounding music.

"Do you still want to go to the jazz club?" She didn't want to now, but was just checking with Ian.

"No, let's get out of here!" Ian yelled over the crowd. He was itching to leave and was feeling hungry.

"There's a good Indian restaurant at the next train stop, Hollywood Curry," said Annie. "Penchant was filming in this area just a few months ago," she commented, proudly. "We go this way. We just have to take the train further downtown." She felt better having a friend with her, instead of the loneliness of waiting for the train by herself.

Again reassuring him, "It's just a ride on the Metro there. Doesn't take too long," she said, hoping he wasn't bored. They unlinked their arms because they didn't like people staring at them. Shoulder to shoulder, she liked the feeling of his sturdy arms pressed against her slender ones. He was silent, frowning a bit, but those piercing brown eyes and his bright blonde hair made an impression on her.

Walking out of the Metro to the stop nearest their destination, they linked arm in arm again, with Annie leading the way. "It's just a short walk to the restaurant. They have the most amazing Indian food," she gushed. They chose a cozy wooden booth and smelled the aroma of spices and yogurt dressing, their stomachs beginning to growl with hunger and anticipation.

He confided, under his breath, "You know, when I first saw

43

you, you were wearing a lowcut flower top, exposing your cleavage. I really liked how you were unafraid to dress differently."

Amused, she said, under her breath, "I don't have any cleavage. I'm really small up there." As if in a daze, he lowered his voice again.

His dark brown eyes pierced Annie's soul again, and she started to feel like a teenager, with even more of a crush on him. He thought he had better discuss work before getting too involved with her. He had a secret he didn't want Annie to know about. Not yet.

"So I was really glad our legal department handled the companies' merger so well," he spoke, clearing his throat. He wanted to separate the business end of it with the emotions he was feeling. "There was no drama, I just remember the producers at both production houses making an agreement to work together instead of competing with each other."

She agreed. "I was kind of afraid I would lose my job, but Laura told me they're keeping everyone on. If it wasn't for your legal team we might have been in hot water financially over all of this." Then another one of his deep stares and shining deep brown eyes. There was a whisper of a smile on his lips.

As if in a trance, he fixed his eyes on hers and said, "I could so fall in love with you now."

Annie was charmed. She smiled so much during dinner her facial muscles couldn't relax. She had never really had this type of reaction before from anyone. He continued to talk to her, gazing into her dark brown eyes, like he was under a spell.

"I have a girl… Back where I'm from. In Huntington Beach."

"A girl, you said?"

"She's taking care of my cat." His voice trailed off.

Maybe the cat sitter he hired, said Annie to herself. But why would he say that to me, now?

They continued eating their dinner, with just the right amount of curry sauce to dip the fresh Naan bread in. The sweet and sour yogurt sauce complimented the flatbread perfectly. Lentils and chickpeas in the recipes filled their hungry stomachs and nourished them with thoughts of hugs and kisses.

"This food is really good," said Ian, and she shared her dream with him. "I'd love to sell my screenplay, that is, when it's good and ready, to a production house. I just have to talk to the right people." She felt she could tell Ian anything.

"When *you're* good and ready," he emphasized. "You just need more confidence in yourself," he said, with measured words and looks.

"I forgot to talk to the screenwriting team at the wrap party. I was so afraid it would never be the right time and I would get the brush-off," she opened up.

"Don't worry about it, you'll know when it's time. And don't take rejection personally," he added.

Annie felt so sure of herself when she was around Ian. She felt compelled to reach over and grab his hand, but she resisted that urge, just admiring his gaze and short, cropped hair. She was surprised at this. This vulnerability that she had never felt before. Her face got hot, heart beating more, and she beamed at him.

That was an understatement. No one had ever said those kind of words to her before. Not to casual dating Annie. Not Annie the other woman. She didn't think anything about what this might lead to. She was just as entranced as he was, and didn't want to break that spell.

After dinner, they took the train at the subway station to the stop near her home. Reaching the gate to her condo unit in Santa Monica, she turned to look at Ian.

"That was really fun," she said, cheerfully. "I'm glad we chose that place to have dinner. I didn't want to get lost in that crowd. I was hungry …."

She fidgeted with her keys. "Well, I guess I'll see you around, maybe at Dan's place?" she said, almost coyly. Ian replied, "Yeah, I'd like that. I had a good time, too." She turned, then closed the door behind her. Proud of herself for resisting the urge to kiss him, she really wanted to set a record for herself to not go blindly into a relationship based on passion alone.

The next eight weeks both of them thought about each other, a few dates at a Chinese restaurant that served gourmet food from Szechuan, walking along the seashore at Santa Monica Beach, a five-minute drive from Annie's condo, while talking over some of their dreams and hopes for the future.

"I always watch the credits when the screen rolls at the end of movies. I've been told that screenwriters don't get much compensation for their work, but to me they should get top billing, along with the actors," she said. She remembered how Bill made a sarcastic comment on how the story people, the writers get next to nothing while the stars get a bulk of the income. Very pessimistic. "It could be true, but I love what I do."

When Ian brought up the idea to see a movie together, she was quick to tell him about a charming independent movie theater in their neighborhood that showed arthouse movies and rare retro films. The film currently playing was a joint venture of Spanish and American production companies. A comedy-drama, it was written by a well-known director from New York City. They held hands throughout most of the movie, enjoying each others' company.

The following week, they stopped by Retro Records Café, a record store and restaurant where the wireless computer crowd went to buy coffee and listen to live music.

The African-American folk and rock singer smiled at Annie and Ian as he sang "In My Life" by the Beatles, while they sat beside each other on the cushy sofa. When he got to the lines "In my life, I love you more," Annie looked over at Ian and held his hand. She sensed he looked bored or worried. But she thought he looked even more cute, laughing silently to herself. They were both like little kids experiencing love for the first time. He was quiet and seemed to have something troubling on his mind.

She leaned back and relaxed. This was her time off from work.

Her relaxation time. It was just a short walk to Annie's and at the condo gate afterwards, she turned to face him. Her heart was pounding with excitement. "Would you like to come inside for awhile?" said Annie, softly. He quietly followed her to her door.

Inside, they took off their shoes. "A Chinese household. They always take off their shoes," said Ian. He threw his jacket on the old futon that badly needed replacing. Annie sat on the floor in the living room as Ian sat behind her. She relaxed, surprisingly very open. Their skin touching, Annie's tan and Ian's pale, caused electricity to spark up inside them. And their kiss. Just straight-on, not slobbery wet like some guys. Firm kisses of adoration for each other. He held her in a tight hug, in-between those loving kisses.

Of all the guys she had been meeting, she was attracted to him most. She loved his straight-on, no nonsense attitude about things. She wasn't expecting what came next. A ring on his phone. Was this another woman? His voice was very persistent. She couldn't make out what they were talking about.

After speaking for awhile, he hung up, obviously upset about something. "This woman who I rent a room from... Marissa. She's got her whole family staying there tonight. She's always got these people over, moving in and out. I don't get any privacy. And I tripped in the bathroom at her place. It's a liability! I've got to move out. I could move into your place!"

"No, this place is small for two people. I need space for my studio and my writing," Annie insisted. "I would pay you," he continued. "You'd have more than enough money for dinners out and to pay your bills!" "I don't think it would work out. I can't really rent this place," Annie said, a bit disappointed herself. "There's really not enough room here…," her voice trailing off.

Ian started to get more nervous. Why he was so desperate she didn't know. I guess if I had roommate problems I'd be in the same shoes, she thought to herself. "Look–I have to move out, now!" he said, frantically.

"Ian, do some looking around to find the best place for you," she said, firmly. She picked up a pillow and clasped it close to her belly. She was holding it like she wished she could hold Ian, just to calm him down.

Then calmly, he said, "Annie, I wanna see you this weekend." But it was the unspoken acceptance of their relationship, their friendship, that made the most sense, besides his expression of attraction.

The two enjoyed each other's company, as no one else had that same sense of humor. And they loved to watch movies together. Like her, he was a big film buff and knew something about how films were made. He put on a DVD copy of the classic sci-fi movie, "Bladerunner" and took it all in with her.

Not that this was the genre she wrote in. It was just a welcome diversion. And it made her happier she was a romantic comedy writer. She felt the long-missed comfort of her arm wrapped around another's arms. At least watching this movie would take their mind off of things.

She would have to do some talking to friends about this, she thought. It just might help to open up and share. Or was she just going to boast about it?

She was in love and just wanted to shout it to the rooftops. Ian, however, was adamant about baring his personal life among friends no matter how close they happened to be. She liked to share her problems about relationships, just to see what she could learn to improve it.

Maybe I should keep it to myself more, she thought as she turned it over in her mind.

But no, she was swayed for only that one second. What are friends for, anyway?

Chapter Six

                    KATE
          Hey, don't want to bother
          you again, but remember
          this is a special day?

                    JOSH
          Yeah.

Josh is engaged in his work.

                    KATE
          This is our tenth
          anniversary of meeting
          each other.

Josh is still reading on his iPad.

                    KATE
          Hello. Are you listening?
          Earth to Josh.

The following week Ian and Annie resisted themselves for as long as they could, but it seemed to only make them closer.

One particular Saturday, they agreed to get together again.

"Hey...I'm here," he said on his cell as he waited outside the gate to her condo. She came out in a jean skirt, a lace lavender top and matching heels. Courtesy of ordering for the thousandth time from Ladies Secret online. She must be their best customer. More than a few times she ordered almost every month, for on sale items.

Once the packages piled up so high it took up the whole space of their sofa when she went back to living with her parents a few yers ago before she got the production job. More hoarding. She knew she had to work on that.

But she couldn't walk at all down the sloped sidewalk in those horrible, though good-looking in a way, high heels. She wanted to look nice, and didn't think twice about it, despite her middle-aged feet. She just managed to side-step awkwardly near the shrubbery, in a squat position just to avoid landing on her face, and met Ian. Hope no one spied on me, she panicked. A woman parked in a car nearby burst out laughing and pointed out Annie to her fellow passenger. She was really trying, but she really *could not* wear those heels.

Ian liked checking her out. "I think you get dressed like this just to get my reaction. You're a little seductress."

"No, I'm not," she defended herself, almost childishly as she hid her enthusiasm. He draped an arm over Annie as they both walked back to her place. Safe inside, where onlookers couldn't laugh at her trying to walk well in those shoes, Annie and Ian sat on the futon sofa.

As if to change the subject, he said, "I wanna see your art." She let him see a spiral bound sketchbook of her artwork. Her paintings were sparkling fairy figures in all colors of the rainbow.

Turning the pages, he remarked, "Beautiful!" he said. "You're so creative, you have achieved so much." The well-proportioned figures looked animated, after she drove herself with pencil and bold strokes of watercolors to get them to look that way. He turned his gaze to the impressionistic landscapes floral arrangements she had painted and were framed around her apartment. "You're so creative," he remarked.

"Do you ever sell these?"

"I've sold a few, here and there," she replied, pouring some sparkling water with lime juice for them.

"You've got potential, I can see that," he said, as they sipped from their glasses. "You should really market your work."

In the evening after a homemade dinner that Ian had prepared this time, she dressed for comfort in her light blue fleece pajamas. It was much too warm for the California weather, but it made her feel cozy. "Are those baby pajamas?" he asked, almost innocently.

She hugged Ian for saying that, then reached for a well-worn paperback on the table. Ian listened as he sat next to her.

Opening up the book, she relayed what she was reading. "My Chinese astrology book says the marriage combination between a Rooster sign, that's you--and me--an Ox...you and me are a match made in heaven....if you believe in the Chinese zodiac," said

Annie.

"Really?" his face brightening up. "I *like* the Chinese zodiac!" he said as he relaxed next to her. She knew it was just superstition. Maybe something in it could be true…

He lay back on the couch, facing the ceiling. "Annie MacDrew. Annie MacDrew," he daydreamed out loud.

"What are you saying?" she said, smiling. They held each other close. Couldn't resist each other, charming as they were to each other.

"Annie, you make me so happy." He pulled away from her. "I think we're both lonely." Annie was charmed. He's being cute again, she thought.

Then it happened, a kiss on her cheek and then more. He began kissing her slender neck. She knew she was falling for him. He put his arms around her waist and lifted her, carrying her to the bedroom. She was thrilled by this, and he let his emotions flow with this warmth they felt for each other. "You're a hot woman, Annie …" and he did make her feel hot. She was feeling attached to him. But she was testing the waters.

All I need is a good cool shower to snap out of this, she thought. So she wouldn't let her passions get away with her.

She pulled away abruptly, then turned on the water to the shower and stepped in, welcoming the refreshing water soaking her skin, as she sang to herself. He waited for her to finish, then took one himself. OK, she's not so desperate, he thought. That's what I like about her.

At the kitchen table, he asked, nonchalantly, "What's for dinner?"

"Chicken", she said, opening the meat drawer in the refrigerator. He stood near the kitchenette.

"Ugh," he said, smelling the stench coming from there. "That's all spoiled. You can't keep raw chicken in the fridge for that long. And refreezing already thawed chicken doesn't make the chicken taste good at all."

Embarrassed at her error, but grateful he had explained it, she tossed it into the garbage can. She took out another two breasts of chicken. She was no gourmet cook, and was still learning at her age, but when she was in a good mood her culinary creations turned out well.

"Now what did you mean when you said, you have a girl?" Annie's mind went back to the skillet. And what she had heard him say on their first date.

He was silent for a pause. Then a few seconds later he said, not wanting to tell her, "I have a *girl*......" he paused, reluctantly, "....friend."

She stopped suddenly, and the bowl she had in her hand dropped on the floor. Flashbacks from her past relationship karma flittered in her mind. The guy she had a fling with who had a girlfriend. The waiter who was interested in her, but she found out he was married.

Always the "other woman", she thought, once the initial shock wore off. Back to the present. "You what?! I thought you meant, you have a friend, who happens to be a girl, taking care of your cat!" She took a moment to process it more in her mind. "What's her name?" She anxiously and wearily paused for the answer, her expression waning.

"Piper." He knew he hadn't been honest with her, and replied with humility, head bowed at the dining room table.

"How old is she?"

Another few seconds of silence. "54," he said, softly, but truthfully.

Quietly calculating in her mind, she said, emphatically, "She's fifteen years older than you....why didn't you tell me?" Ian was quiet, trying to stay calm.

"I was dating someone else, too," she opened up, when she came to her senses. "Jim. I met him at a Clutter therapy group. Because I had too much stuff I bought and didn't really need. He bought these for me," she said, as she went to the closet, dug around and held up the pair of electric blue high-heeled shoes to show him. "Because I wanted them. But they're not good for me. They hurt my feet." And she told him that she couldn't walk straight in them because it threw her back out of alignment.

"I like you in flat shoes better," he retorted. He took out a DVD from his bag. "Here, this is a *good movie*. 'Romancing of the Stone'". Ian put the DVD deftly into the player and sat back on the sofa. He pointed out the scene where Kathleen Turner wears high heels in the jungle and Michael Douglas takes her shoes to break the heels off. "Look! See? You can't walk in those heels!"

She made a mental note of it, but she had her mind on other things.

After the movie was over, she was straight with him. "If you have a girlfriend, maybe we better not see each other," she said, still hurting from his not being honest with her. After a minute, she calmed down, sitting next to him on the floor. Ian walked closer to the television. He leaned his head in her lap, while she stroked his hair. Annie offered to show a short film that she acted in, a class project. She had a small part in the movie as a professor. Ian arched his neck to look closer to the screen. "You're really photogenic, do you know that?"

She turned over what he had said in her mind.

"Annie, if it wasn't for Piper, I'd be putting that ring on your finger." He gazed into her eyes. "Really?" she paused. She was shocked. She had never received a marriage proposal, outside of a man she had a crush on who she found out later was gay. "Sure would be weird finding him in bed one morning with another man," a friend had said to her.

"But you have a girlfriend." She wanted him to face up to the truth, and she knew she had to, also. She stopped stroking his hair. "Maybe you better go home," she said to Ian, realizing the situation she was in. Maybe she should start out with a clean slate. "What if Piper came after me and threatened me?" she said, hastily.

"No, she's not like that," he said, slightly annoyed. Not likely, but she was starting to panic a little inside.

He responded to her comment. "No, I wanna spend time with

you," he said, with a youthful voice that showed the little boy inside, trying to get out of himself. He was sincerely attracted to her as if she wasn't like any other woman he knew of, and with boyish abandon, he went back to laying in her lap. Her ego was flattered, but she knew she shouldn't just take the compliment.

Always the "other woman", she thought again, once the initial shock wore off. She shouldn't be too easy on Ian for this. Again, she thought it over. He was spoken for already. But she couldn't help it, she was falling for him, too. I just can't send him home, she thought.

Chapter Seven

At Penchant, her good friend and former screenwriting classmate, Ogbay, stopped by the studio. Smiling reassuringly, he was an optimistic African man looking to pitch his own screenplay to anyone concerned, who greeted her with, "Hello. How are you, Miss Annie Chen?" his dark face beaming with good charm and humor.

She answered enthusiastically, "Fine, how are you doing, my friend? So, do you have a girlfriend, yet?" She poked at him for fun. "I have lots of girlfriends! Girls love me." More laughter from Ogbay.

She teased back. "Well! Men love me!" They both laughed, just pretending they were glamorous movie stars. Annie opened up with more dialogue. This time, seriously.

"This guy I've been seeing. I've only known him two weeks and he wants to share my apartment with me. He says it would save me rent and he'd have a temporary place to stay." She paused, even more seriously. "I'm not sure I want someone to boss me around in my own place. I like my independence. And on top of that, he has another girlfriend!" she said, bewildered.

"You better think that over. You don't have to decide right away," and she nodded in agreement. "Don't complain about him to me. He might want to stay longer and get attached to his landlady." Ogbay slyly laughed.

Smiling, she said, "O.K. I won't have you say, 'I told you so.'"

She shared some of her background as a writer with Ogbay, sometimes unsure how to advance, writing-wise and how to find an agent. "Keep writing, you'll find a way to market your work as you go along, and keep getting familiar with what you are writing about. Don't talk about your ideas, except when you are pitching to a movie producer or agent."

Annie was proud of him as a friend who had worked on various productions in the Los Angeles area. They had read some screenplay scenes together to see what worked or didn't work in their scriptwriting. He also offered brotherly advice on relationships.

"You've got to allow time for this to develop," he said, but not preaching to her about Ian. "You'll find out if you want this to happen." His voice got more serious. "Don't always rely on what your family may say about it." She took this home with her and brooded over her situation. Annie still wanted to be friends with Ian, but was torn over what some members of her family would think about their relationship. They knew how many times she was disappointed.

Back at her desk, she reviewed which script revisions she had to send over to Gayle. "O.K.," she said, facing Gayle. "Here's the changes made for Act 2 of "Take Me Away". I made several copies, do you need more?" After Gayle received the paperwork from her, she told her, "You have nothing to worry about now, Annie. Bill's been charged with sexual misconduct."

Annie's jaw dropped. She couldn't form any words for this.

"Hard to believe, huh? Or maybe, that does sound like something he would do. A colleague of mine went to the police. Laura told me Bill is facing up to 30 years in prison, 10 if he has a good lawyer. "He told everyone he wants to be working again after all that.

When Annie asked what job he wanted, she answered, "According to Laura and Dan, he wants to be in retail sales. Wholesales for ladies undergarments. Like Freida's of Hollywood, you know what I mean?""Wow, that's just up his alley," she said, as she grinned, happy he was out of the picture. "I'm glad he wants to find something more suited to his tastes. He probably would've caused more mayhem at Nine Figure Pictures. That is, after he served his term." She was still in shock over that news. But thinking it over, she said, "Well that was a nice surprise!"

They were both glad to change the subject. Calmly, Gayle asked, "What about Ian, how has it been working out with him? Ian the law clerk." She immediately thought she shouldn't have mentioned this to Gayle. It must have slipped out one time. Annie wasn't expecting to spill the news on her relationship. She probably should have been more quiet about it. Turning this over with herself for the gazillionth time, she calmed herself down.

"It's O.K. It's fine. I just didn't expect the competition. He's engaged to someone now. Someone who he knew before he met me. I found out about that, I think it's really better to let him go. But every time I do this, I find myself wanting him even more…and…"

"Wait, wait," Gayle motioned with her hands, "I would see how this goes for you. In my experience, I just let things happen naturally. Sometimes the guy left, but with my guy, he stuck with me, chose me over someone else he was dating, you do remember from last time we talked about it? We had a talk and I told him I really didn't want to see anyone else, and that we could work out our differences, because ours was a better match. And I didn't feel guilty about it. Maybe you're holding that in.

"You deserve the best guy for you, Annie."

Annie slept on it, going over all of this in her mind.

Chapter Eight

```
           KATE
I think I need a break.
I'll call my sister and
spend time with her.
I haven't seen her for
a year.

           JOSH
Yeah, that's fine. Just
don't complain about
our relationship.
```

The next week Annie invited her sister Kay to the Chinese noodle restaurant, Hunan Fusion, for lunch. A local restaurant that had a hint of elegance without too extravagant prices, Annie had been there with Ian once. Kay, who was a bit rebellious against the status quo, with those long locks of silver and pepper hair rolled into a bun, and was a grassroots activist who was always signing petitions, and in the past had asked for signatures while working for Planet Peace.

She was unlike Annie, never thinking of dying her hair, wearing makeup or fancy clothing. When asked about her political stance, she knew where she stood, veering on the far left, and you wouldn't want to get in an argument with her.

She must have noticed those blue heels in the back of Annie's car. "I think you should stop wearing those high heels. They're so bad for you. I'm even getting foot problems myself," she said, looking down at her sneakers. Her Sketchers sneakers weren't exactly athletic or arch supportive, either.

"You're probably right," she responded, her brow furrowed, a bit embarrassed. Annie realized her older sister Kay genuinely wanted to help her, and Kay didn't like it if she thought someone was trying to take advantage of her younger sister. So that was going good, Annie realized. This whole thing about her dating experiences proved that.

Annie wanted to open up to her. "I know, Kay. This guy I'm dating … he has a girlfriend. He told me later she works as a coat checker at a bar in Huntington Beach."

"How can he have two girlfriends?" she remarked, as if it was beyond her belief. "It's really hard to get rid of people if they move in," she said, matter-of-factly.

Annie tried to stop herself, but she couldn't hold it in.

"He was even talking about marriage!" Annie blurted. OK, this isn't complaining, it's just me, being honest, she realized, in a quick flash of defense.

"Really?" She too was surprised. "Kenneth didn't propose

until after two years of us dating together. Isn't that rushing things?" Kay slowly mixed together her hoisin sauce on top of the thin mushu pancake.

Annie took a few bites of the lightly spiced General Tso's chicken over rice.

"And he has a girlfriend," Kay paused, then went back to swallowing a bite of her mushu pork pancake. "But don't feel sorry for him. Be a little mean to him, even," she said, firmly.

"I don't feel sorry for him! And I don't want to be mean to him!" A pause again. Maybe I shouldn't have told her, Annie stopped herself, as she finished a savory Chinese green onion pancake.

Kay put her finger to her mouth and shushed Annie so the whole restaurant wouldn't hear. She changed the subject. Smiling, she recounted, "Remember when we all ate here for Mom's birthday, and you gave her a watercolor painting. It was a small one," she indicated the length and width with her hands, "but it was really cute. A fairy painting in watercolor."

Annie had to think a minute about that. "Oh, you mean the Asian fairy painting I did last year, or a few years ago?" Annie was excited and feeling blessed she had a good sister who supported her artistic endeavors. She relaxed more, and asked, "How is your own illustration coming along? I remember you showed me your portfolio." A black hand-carved linoleum block print on cream colored paper was the illustration that came to her mind. Kay had shown it to her once, more than once, with children sitting and playing around a campfire. "You could write and illustrate it yourself, maybe get it self-published.

"Or maybe I could find a writer," she smiled, cocked her head and pointed to Annie. "Yes!" Annie raised her voice. She was so excited about that prospect. But I'm up to my ears in this screenplay. She thought for a moment. Then, without hesitation, she decided, "I'll do it! After I finally sell a script, I hope to have more free time, and that's a great idea!" she decided, confident in herself.

"O.K. Annie," beamed Kay. She always maintained her moral support for her relatives, and encouraged Annie with her artistic element.

"Don't forget, next week we get together for dinner. With Mom and Dad. And our friends," said Kay, in between eating the savory black bean mushu sauce, cabbage and carrots mix.

Annie brightened. "Alright, that'll be fun," finally relaxing as she enjoyed the fried pancake. She always did enjoy dinner with her family. Sure, she had conflicts that were ego-based and there were culture clashes, generational obstacles to face up to and overcome, her mom and dad's different ideas on who would be best for Annie's future. "I love all of my family," she added, with a smile.

The minute Kay mentioned family get togethers, Annie relaxed and felt their warm support. They could all feel that from her, and they gave back in many ways, from the sweet bean cakes for the Autumn Moon Festival to pork siu mai for Chinese new years'. They loved her, no matter what she did.

As for Ian, he had this problem to deal with. Piper wouldn't let up. She called Ian often, and Ian was beset with phone calls from her, sometimes checking his every move.

He listened to the voicemails on his phone. "Ian, this is Joe, Joe Palmer, can you meet with the firm Wednesday to discuss the loose ends we need to tie up so we can get this merger going? Alright, give me a call."

Next up, he gave a listen to Piper, her domineering, insistent voice sharply reminded him, "Ian, you forgot to send me the money….what's wrong with you? You said you would send me $400 a month! You know I told you the air conditioner needed to be replaced in this dump," as she forced the window open which was painted over too much and was hard to open. They lived in a cheap rental, and it showed with the broken-down conditions they lived in.

In between her low paying job she almost harassed him daily by phone, and once she got him on the line, she would go over her list of demands. "You were going to buy me that outfit I saw online. They have it in the store, Rodeo Drive. I told you about this a month ago and you did nothing for me," Piper growled, when she finally got Ian over the phone. "You know you can afford it. And you know how I love classy clothes," she said, her flirtatious voice rolling off of her tongue, manipulating him.

Ian would roll his eyes and nod, "OK, OK…I'll get there this weekend. I've got to work now, Joe Palmer is meeting with me overtime about that merger. I have a deadline."

Can't that wait? Hey, I thought you were getting a raise?! I want that pretty pink lowcut dress, that minidress , the one in the Louis Vuitton store I saw online!" she said, urgently.

"I haven't got a raise, Piper. You're imagining things."

"Oh lord, you promised me that would happen!" she insisted.

"Isn't that kind of dress a little too young for you? I mean, you're 54…."

"And what do you mean by that, Ian? Are you trying to insult me?!" she flew in a rage over his last remark. Then this one took the cake for Piper.

"You're starting to get varicose veins," Ian came back with this. "You need a dress and maybe some leggings to cover that up."

Oh, my lord!" she slapped her forehead. "You are really overstepping the line. Don't you remember my father had everything to do with you getting that job at the law firm," she prattled on. Even though there wasn't an ounce of truth in that.

"Piper, I got a referral for this job from a friend of Joe Palmer. That friend is another law clerk. It had nothing to do with your dad."

"I don't care. And at my age now, that means you better hightail it over there and get me that dress before I get much older!" she blasted on.

"Alright, alright….," he sighed. "Later, I'll talk to you later," trying his best to calm her down.

Annie, oblivious to these demands, thought Piper must be pretty devoted and invested in their relationship. She's probably pining away, saying how much she misses him. Very carefully, she gave him these words. "Ian, I need to let you, know, I've been thinking it over and, we really shouldn't see each other. You've got Piper…"

Ian stopped her. "I know, I know, I understand," tired because she had gone back and forth about this a million times.

"Well, maybe I'll see you at the office," Annie said. "We can be good friends, I think that's best." Annie felt relieved of any shame that was caused by Ian being in a relationship already.

"Yeah, I get it," he said, disappointed. His head was reeling from all of Piper's demands. He really did like Annie. She was thoughtful and most of the time, gentle. She didn't make unnecessary demands on him. Annie knew that she better mind her own business. But she was in too deep to kick him out of her life. Even if some of her friends told her to kick him to the pavement.

She just couldn't do it. Every time she tried to break up, she felt something was missing. There was something about him that filled the emptiness she felt, after other men left her by herself, once they got a quick fix of the "goods" she supposedly was providing them. She was always uncomfortable about that.

After the second two weeks apart, Ian was over again at her place. Out of the blue, he flirted with her over another fantasy of his. "You know what you look like. You look like Lynda Carter.

You're Wonder Woman!" he said, while squeezing her shoulder arm and sneaking in a kiss.

Annie was a little dumbstruck hearing this statement, which was truly off the mark according to her. She just laughed, knowing it was his imagination.

"You're cute when you say that. I never compared myself to Wonder Woman," as Ian stripped down to his birthday clothes and examined his stomach in the mirror. The condo unit was full of mirrors, around each of the two bathrooms, maybe because it was built in the wild 1980's.

"I'm getting fat," he said as he looked at himself sideways. I'm just a fat fuck."

"Nooo, you're not so bad, Ian. A little pudginess is fine. See look, I'm chubby here, too!" She rubbed her belly. Ian locked eyes with Annie. He was poised in a position of almost pouncing on her, when the vision of Piper came to him. In his imagination she was scolding him, berating him to let Annie be. He was about to consider taking a cold shower as soon as possible.

Then came a knock at Annie's door. Ian quickly reached for his underwear and jeans. "Who could *that* be?" he said. "Did you invite a guy over?" he whispered beneath his breath, urgently.

"No, are you kidding?" she whispered back, annoyed. He dressed quickly, back in his dark jeans and T-shirt, and she threw a robe on, then walked quickly to the door to take a look through the peephole.

Chapter Nine

```
            JOSH
You need to get control
of yourself. You know, all
that spending you're
doing.

            KATE
I know, I know. Now you're
nagging me.

            JOSH
I'm only looking out for
you. Kate, you have a
hoarding problem. Get
rid of all this stuff.
```

The postman left a large box. She opened it, which contained a lot of luscious and colorful, sexy underwear, from Ladies Secret. She didn't remember her mail ordering this. As if she had put it out of her mind.

"What are you doing? Who was that?" he asked, from the

other room. She put on a lacy light blue bra, then looked at herself in the mirror. "Just trying something on. It's nothing, really. This is silly." She squeezed her flab in front of the mirror. Better get in some exercise. And not pushups.

"It's skimpy underwear," he said as he held some panties and bras up to the light. "Annie, you can't afford this stuff. Like me, I really want an Xbox."

"You don't need it," she rebounded, quickly. As if to justify her own weakness. She just loved those catalogs. And getting those surprises in the mail.

"I can't afford it! My friends said, 'Dude, you can't buy that stuff!'" He paused, then remarked, "I think you just buy all that to make yourself feel better." She knew he was right. Makeup and clothes. She had a closet and cabinets overflowing with products to make her "feel good." Stuff with perfume, which she was allergic to. Sheepishly, she got back into her clothes.

"Yeah, you're right. I'm glad you care about me. No one else seems to."

"Annie, you've got a lot of people who care about you."

He reached out and gave her a hug saying, "I just keep thinking about you, Annie," as he opened up. "Maybe I'm learning, but Annie...." His voice trailed off. Annie, almost hesitating, finished the sentence. "But I think we better not see each other."

"You say that and then you miss me!" She agreed, not very eagerly, "I know."

Ian changed the subject. "In high school, I never went out on dates."

Annie remarked, "Neither did I. I was a nerd!" she laughed. Without waiting for his response to that, she focused on him, so she didn't feel embarassed. "Really? I find that hard to believe. You're really handsome. Has anyone ever told you that?" she asked, as they lounged together on the floor.

"Yeah, my first two girlfriends." He put his arm around Annie and hugged her. "You are so hot, so talented. I love our relationship. You're a beautiful Asian woman."

"Stop talking to me like that! We're just friends now!" she lashed back, removing his arms from around her shoulders. She knew what that might lead to, so she had to push him away. She wanted to unemotionally resist him.

"I love our friendship! I love the chemistry between us," he continued. "You know in some societies men have more than one wife."

Annie, not believing a word he just said, retorted, "You're dreaming. So that's how you see me, as a second wife? I mean, who wants to be second best?" Annie shook her head at this presumptuous figment of his imagination. Ian changed the subject again. He knew better than to push her buttons like that.

"I like glasses. They're sexy," he said, as he looked up and touched her glasses. Then he withdrew for a moment. "Piper might call me back tonight."

Without really giving it a second thought, Annie blurted out, "Leave her, now! It's either her, or me!" She raised her voice at this, indignant. Immediately, Annie began to feel uncomfortable. The words that came out were *not* the words she intended to feel or express. But she was tired of feeling like she was the other woman. That she was only second best.

Quickly, he retorted, "Please don't say that! I'm not leaving Piper. I can't do that to her." Annie frowned. "You women get so dumb. Once you give one kiss to them, they're thinking, 'O.K. when are we getting married?'"

"We're not dumb," she made it clear. "Some men are dumb, too." He gave up on trying to relay something to her about that.

Just then, another ring on his cell. Ian walked into the other room. "Yeah, hi…I'm over at the new place. I just had to get out of there. Too many people invading my privacy. So how's MacGregor doing?"

Piper, an attractive light-haired brunette, with a trim figure, was lying in bed in a shiny, purple satin robe. "Oh, he's doing great. He misses you. You know, I had to get rid of those ugly tomato vines you planted in our place. Too many little red ants around."

"Those tomato plants took hours to grow. How could you throw them out?" Ian's voice was sinking.

"Oh I know, you really liked them, Ian, but I live here too, you know…I just called to say I'll be needing the money we talked about last month."

"I just sent you $500 a few days ago, Piper! What did you do with all that money?"

"Where is the money going, you ask? I told you, it's for groceries and food," she lied. "No, I mean it, you know I like fancy food and eating out....what's that? Am I eating out alone? None of your business! Hey you owe it to me because you borrowed money from me to buy beer! What's that? I'm lying? I'm having a friend come over in a few, so I don't have time to talk anymore now."

"Is it a guy?" Ian asked, woefully.

Overhearing this, Annie's first reaction was that this woman was trying to control and take over his life. She accepted her feelings, angry at the way Piper was treating him. Why is Ian staying with her? She turned this over in her mind.

"Well, what if it *is* a guy?" Piper continued, defensively. "Ian, we went over this. I'm not married to you. I'm allowed to have my 'male admirers'....Ian, you're being an asshole now....we're not married!" She smiled impishly and laughed. "Did you get close to this *friend*?" he demanded. "Ian, you're my number one, what made you think that?!"

"Piper, we're supposed to be serious about each other...what is going on there?" Ian replied, flustered.

"Hey, I gotta go, he's expecting me any minute now," she said, hastily. "Alright, *later,*" Ian said, louder. He wasn't too pleased.

Piper hung up the phone. Immediately after this, she raided the closet they shared, opening the door so hard the wardrobe shook and Ian's clothes fell around in disarray. Looking at a white shirt and blue patterned tie that belonged to him, she was convinced her friend Chuck would look perfect in it.

This friend, sitting right there on Ian and Piper's couch, helped himself to dinner out of a Chinese food carton. He laughed to himself as Piper remarked, "Hey babe, how do you think this will look like on you? Your abs are in much better shape than Ian's." She held up the starched white shirt and laid it on top of his shirtless six-pack abs. He sat forward, still laughing and slipped it over his smooth biceps.

"How's this?" he asked, as Piper slyly said, "Looks a hundred times better on *you*, Chuck!" and gave him a smooth tongue kiss. "He'll never miss that, and these pants. He hardly ever dresses up." She laughed along with him. "Fits better than on that fat stomach of his."

The outfit was something she got for Ian on his birthday. She wasn't having any luck with increasing her pay with more hours after they cut them back at the nightclub because she was discovered stealing some of the nightclub owner's clothing on the job.

If she hadn't used her feminine charms on him she probably would have been out of that job in a minute. To be sure, she never did tell her boss where his belongings were. And Piper didn't want to spend any extra money on gifts. "Ian never wears this, it's too dressy," she said to Chuck, as she continued rummaging through his wardrobe. "I'll just take this one, and that shirt for you, Ian won't ever notice," as Chuck laughed to himself again.

Ian was in the living room again. "I wanna watch this samurai movie with you, Annie," as he held up the DVD for her to see.

They were like two young people, wrapped up in warm blankets, huddled in front of the TV. Ian turned on her DVD and put in "The Forbidden Castle." Reaching over to where she lay next to him, he extended his arm around her and said, very carefully and calmly, "Annie, I love you."

Despite the conflict in her mind about him and Piper as a couple, she was happy to hear this. No one had ever said those three words to her before. Well, four. It sounded even better with her name attached. Love was still a game to her. She felt jaded, although through it all she did find his talk about love to be an honest one.

Cheerfully she replied, "I love you, too, Ian." She said it as if it was singing. She was so happy to hear it from him that her reaction almost came off as not being serious enough.

Chapter Ten

        KATE
Is there someone else?

Josh pauses, looking solemn.

        JOSH
I'm sorry I didn't tell
you. It's just that, I
was attracted to you.

Kate rolls her eyes.

Back at the office, Ogbay and Annie had a good talk about what had been going on lately in their worlds. Ogbay teased Annie like a brother would to a sister. "You can't resist your hot young tenant…he can't resist you, a hot landlady!"

She was jovial but fielded Ogbay's assumptions, as she raised her voice, "Stop! He hasn't moved in. I'm just not meeting anyone else," she said, looking a bit sad. He replied in all sincerity, "Why don't you have some faith in yourself? That's all you need."

Something in what he said caused Annie to make a shift inside of herself. She had awhile to think about this. "I think I'll feel better seeing my sister and our family's friends when we join them for dinner together." Ogbay nodded and put his hands on his knees.

"You just need to make a change in the way you look at this man. You got to make that change in yourself." She agreed. Ogbay always had something wise to talk to her about. Or joke with her about. She looked forward to having dinner together with Kay, like all of her family. She knew she would always find acceptance and love among their familiar faces.

"I just hope I can find some middle ground with my sister," she shared with him.

"When *you* are happy, *they* will be happy, you see?" And Annie nodded in accord to this. "Now get to work on that script of yours, Annie."

Chapter Eleven

The next afternoon, Kay came by Annie's to get ready for the dinner. She drove near the sidewalk to meet her and patiently waited in the car. "Annie, is there something bothering you?" she asked, while Annie swung over to the passenger seat in the car, trying to calm her older sister's nerves. "Like that guy, Ian, who was going to move in?" Her voice was filled with concern for her sister.

"No. He hasn't moved in." Annie knew where that conversation was leading to, so she kept her peace. She knew she had been complaining all along to Kay about Ian. That wasn't going to help much. They passed sparkling lakes and views of the Santa Monica mountains while Annie remained silent most of the time. They parked a block from their childhood friend's home in Westlake Village, where the family and friends from Michigan that now lived in the Los Angeles area got together to catch up on what everyone was doing, or should be doing, as was usually the agenda of the older generation.

"Here, here! We thought you weren't going to make it! So glad you came!" an energetic Chinese lady, Mrs. Tiao shouted, standing in front of their suburban home, and greeting a friendly hello with her palms. "Judy is just about to finish with those homemade chicken dumplings, so you got here at just the right time, after all," as she continued waving them inside to the living room.

Mrs. Tiao was the mother of their friend, Judy, a young student in the Chinese language school they used to go to when they were all kids. Annie's parents were there, too, sitting patiently waiting at the dining room table. They were all smiles and laughter, listening to Mrs. Tiao's recounts of a humorous encounter between Judy and one of her male friends.

"He really wanted to get closer to her, but Judy, you know my Judy, is so stubborn, she wouldn't have anything to do with him. So what does he do? He threw a slipper at her bedroom window to get her attention and he tried to climb up the tree to climb in…no, he did not make it, he fell backwards and hurt his spine," some of the other parents smiled at this, and some reacted in surprise. They were just having a good time. Their laughter was loud and strong. No one seemed old in their mind or attitude. No one was serious. Except for Mr. and Mrs. Chen.

"Well, you know, our Annie, she has all the bad luck. She just stopped dating that guy, Bill, who was chasing all of the skirts at that company, a few blocks away from the other company where our Annie works," said Mr. Chen. "And for no good reason, all he wanted was *sex*." Annie immediately regretted telling her mother about Bill. The words just slipped out. At this, the other parents in their seventies and eighties gasped and reacted, "Ohhhh, my!"

"Yes, that's true. So I am wary of anyone who wants to date my Annie," Mr. Chen waved his hand across his face as if to brush off the idea of Bill the Bachelor being in his daughter's life again. Annie lowered her eyes and stared at the food, feeling like Allie did. Being with parents sometimes made her feel like a teenager or a young woman again. Oh well. If it kept her feeling young.

She finally got the courage to say, "Dad, you don't need to bring this up. Bill the Bachelor is in the past!" But there was no stopping them. You can't stop people from talking, her friend, Gayle had told her.

"I heard that is the status quo at the movie studios, everyone dating everyone else and breaking up at the drop of a *hat*! I know because I read the biography of Joan Crawford, and...." Annie interjected, "Auntie Julie, that was a long time ago. There's no one like Joan Crawford anymore."

"I don't know about that, I read the facts, like the National Enquirer, you know," Mrs. Tiao said, as Judy came out to the dining area and announced, "OK everybody, the dumplings are *finally* done!" She brought out a large serving platter with the dumplings displayed and Annie helped out with the bowls of dipping sauce.

"What a gre-e-a-t accomplishment, Judy," Mrs. Chen

exclaimed. "Our Annie needs to learn from you. Teach her cooking so she can get her mind off of men like Bill, Bill the Bachelor," as Annie rolled her eyes, and patted her mother on the shoulder.

"Mo-omm, they don't need to know about my love life," groaned Annie.

"Ha! More like your *sex* life!" Annie's mother said, sharply.

"Ohh, wo-o-w! Chen Tai Tai, don't embarrass her!" said Mrs. Tiao, "In front of her friends and ours!" Mrs. Tiao and Mrs. Kung smiled, took a surprised breath in and laughter rocked the room.

"Are you seeing anyone these days, I mean, after that guy Bill as she said?" Mrs. Kung had to ask that. Annie braced herself, saying, "Well yeah, there is a guy. Ian. He's a law clerk helping with the company merger." She half expected one of them, or all of them to shake their heads and scold her for dating someone so soon after Bill the Bachelor. The room went quiet, then slowly and carefully, Mrs. Kung put in her two cents' worth.

"Annie, you know you got to make friends first. Good, solid foundation of friendship. Then you go do what you want. But you, the younger generation cannot wait to take your clothes off and do foolish things. I know, you think I am a proo—a pru--,"

Mrs. Kung leaned over to Mrs. Tiao to help her out, "That's *prude*, Kung Tai Tai, we know the meaning of that one."

"Per-u-u-ude. Yes, you think I am prude…but I know the men want to jump into your pants, and your underwear…and…"

Mr. Chen abruptly stopped her, "Now, Kung Tai Tai, please

get to the point, and don't make it dirty. You know us, we can't stand all of the modern slang and sex words… "

"Just be careful, Annie, we all care for you, so take it easy!" she continued. "Maybe you need vacation to sort out your feelings? Take yourself away from here! You don't have to listen to old farts like us in detail," she paused as Annie and the other generation laughed. "Just in general, protect yourself and your feelings! When you get close to someone you get emotionally involved and it's hard to break up with someone."

Annie felt the concern. Ultimately, she knew she would make the decisions herself. The other younger ladies, daughters of the older generation, like Kung Tai Tai, mostly reacted by their exclamations of "Mom, stop!" and "You don't need to embarrass Annie," or just sat and laughed along with them, enjoying the homemade food.

She knew it would get this way at the dinner parties, all of the elders judging her next move. It seemed to take all of the fun out of dating. She decided to save herself and Ian from potential awkwardness and not say a word about how she felt about Ian.

Chapter Twelve

KATE
My parents are worried
about me.

JOSH
Worried? What are they
worried about?

KATE
They aren't sure about
us. If we're right for
each other.

JOSH
Yeah, I know. I can tell
by the looks they give me
whenever we go out for
dinner with them.

KATE
What does that mean? They're
just concerned and want us
to be happy.

Annie and Ian were hard to separate, despite the warnings from her sister. They were frequent visitors to Café Uno in Santa Monica. And they enjoyed each other's company, like two kids. When they went out for dinner, he reached over to touch her fingers, their hands clasped under the table and their feet were playing footsie with each other.

Giggling to each other, even if the waitress may have been spying on them. I can't resist the huggings and secret kisses when we're alone, she realized. Sometimes I can't even resist it when we're not alone, she mused. He was not like the other guys she knew before. Ian smiled at her and nudged her, shoulder to shoulder. They were that close to each other.

"Walk me to my place?" she asked, wanting to spend more time with him. She knew their time together was limited. She could feel it. It was a blur in her mind. They just fell for each other and somehow felt as if through their instincts, knew they wanted to be together, in private, with no need for words at times. But Annie had to fight that feeling. Ian felt it, too. When they reached the condo common area gate, she turned to look at him. "Hey thanks, I had a really great time," gushed Annie, turning to look at him sideways. I'm glad we're friends." Bravely, he replied, "Yeah, O.K. I don't regret anything."

That was last week. The following week, he called her. I can't stop thinking about you, Annie....I'd like to be with you." Smiling, she said, "OK, laughing softly. We'll see you soon." She was really looking forward to seeing him. Without words between them, she walked downstairs, and turned directly towards the outer gate of her condo. When they rode up the elevator, she stood almost shyly next to him, she was that in love with him. Ian followed her to the door of her apartment.

Once inside, she poured a bubbly drink for both of them in the kitchenette. Turning to offer him a glass, they cheered each other, and he sat back against the pink futon in the living room. She sipped her drink and leaned closer to Ian.

Softly, he said, "You know, Annie, I've been waiting to tell you. I got a raise at my law clerk job. I didn't expect it. They just told me today. Yup, they promoted me."

"Ian, that's wonderful!" she beamed back at him. She had to resist giving him a congratulatory hug. She controlled herself, and was genuinely happy with this turn of events. "I am so glad that things are going so great for you, Ian. You deserve it," she grinned. "You're really believing in yourself."

"*You're* the one that needs to believe in *yourself*," he said, intently trying to get through to her. He wanted to give some of that to Annie. He shook his head, then fixed his eyes on hers. "All I know is you need more confidence in yourself. And good planning, the courage to make your dreams come true!" He lowered his voice, and said, "You gotta take action, Annie. As a talented screenwriter and artist. And someday you're going to make a man really happy."

She looked at him, a little sadly. She wanted it to go on with Ian by her side. She didn't want to see anyone else.

He looked at her, head lowered so he could peer into her eyes. "You know what? You're afraid of commitment. Of giving yourself up to the right guy, *that's* what's up with you. And you work too hard. There's more to life than work. You need to get away from here sometimes."

He stretched his arms out to her. "C'mere, Gimme a hug." They hugged, but she drew away.

"What about Piper?" she pouted.

Ian's face turned stiff as he said, "Piper and I are not married." She seemed unconvinced until he said, "Annie, I've been thinking about you a lot. You're always on my mind, I don't know why." He was falling for her, and never felt those kind of emotions before. Piper was never as close to him in his mind.

He took her soft hand into his own. He stared through her, penetrating her with his desire to hold her. "I'd like to take you away from here for awhile. You know, we could do a day trip somewhere. After my promotion, I found out I can afford that." She never got invites to go anywhere on dates, since she was so busy with work. Maybe that was why she got those one to four night stands.

Instantly, she got an idea. "I know, Ian! Nine Figure Pictures is doing a feature in Carmel, Carmel-by-the-Sea. It's our newest film, 'Take Me Away'. Principal shooting is starting at the first of next month. I've been signed on to work closely with Gayle, our script supervisor. We could spend some time away during lunch break, or after the film shoot ends …"

He closed her mouth with a firm kiss. She continued to speak, "And I told Laura and Dan about us. I think they would be happy to hear about it…" He quickly drew away. A serious change of heart.

"Why'd you have to do *that*," he scowled. She held onto his shoulders. "They won't hurt you," she tried to reassure him.

"No one has to know about this. This is personal. No one has to hear about what we do in private. Annie, you've got friends. Friends who care about you." She smiled, then looked straight at him, with serious intensity.

He continued, his posture straightened up suddenly. He felt it was time to let her know. "Dan told me if he ever saw me trying to date you again, he would not allow me to work with Nine Figure Pictures, now that they combined the two, ever again." He turned his face away, and she saw that handsome profile she couldn't get out of her mind.

"They said that?" She was truly surprised. "That's really drastic." She stared at him and took in his deep brown eyes.

Ian drew his face lower. "Annie, we can't meet like this anymore. They would say I'm taking advantage of you, they know I have a girlfriend. This has never happened to me before." He added that last part because he felt ashamed. Leaning back on the couch, he let his head drop and wrung his hair back, anxiously.

Annie, in defensive mode said, "I'm going to talk to them. They shouldn't be treating you like this."

He felt it was OK to open up to her. "Laura didn't say anything to me when I stopped by the production company last week. Even when I told her the merger was legally solid and wrapped up, when I showed the contract agreement to her," he said. "My reputation is ruined." He paused in silence and hung his head down. "You don't have to have me move in."

"Ian, I can understand you. I was almost out on the streets years ago if it weren't for my friends and family. The image of her moving from different places to another came to life again. That uncomfortable feeling she wanted to push out of her mind. That was when she was a starving English major, trying to exist in the suburbs of Los Angeles.

"It's just that getting back together with you might be like jumping from the frying pan into the fire."

He laughed and said, "I love how you said that."

She continued, more seriously now, "Because you and I would be getting closer together, more than ever. And I have feelings for you. Piper is in love with you." Awkwardly, she let out her feelings, "And I guess I love you. I guess I do. Well, I do. I'm in love with you."

It took a lot to say that. Annie didn't exactly have warm parents or friends that said those sort of things to her while growing up. She couldn't even remember a time when she had said those words to anybody. She was beginning to learn that love *wasn't* a game, if she decided it was based on kindness and true feelings. It was only when she moved to California that she began to open up more. She couldn't continue. Not the way things stood between them. Not with Piper waiting for him to pop the question. But she did care about him, she did love him. Despite the fact he was in a relationship, all that seemed to matter was her undeniable love and attraction to him.

"I love how you said that," Ian smiled. "I'm with you on this. I still think we could get away for awhile, Annie…you need a vacation."

"Even if it is a 'working' vacation?" She fought off the image of them happily together on a romance holiday. "Ian, I don't want to fight with you, but you have a girlfriend. I want to break off our relationship …for good!" she said, her eyes getting teary.

He must have noticed that. "O.K. I understand," he backed off, shaking his head. He had dealt with rejection before. "Well, have a good night, anyway," he mumbled, turned and walked out the door. She watched as he trudged away, hands firmly shoved into his jean pockets, her feelings fighting to stop herself from following him.

Then he quickly turned to face her again. "And Annie? I want you to go out with Jim. Jim seems like a nice guy! It would be your chance to get married."

She responded with, "I don't know. See the thing about him is, I don't really know if I like him or not." "I just don't want you to string him along like that," Ian began. "So are you going to go out with him again?" Annie said, a bit resigned, "OK, I guess so. I will. I'll see you, Ian."

She turned to go inside, while reminding herself, don't

91

underestimate the power of women talking together about their problems and worries. These friendships were very important to her. She was teased as a child by other mean girls that *weren't* her friends, and harassed by inappropriate remarks. She didn't know what to expect every day at school, growing up.

Later, as a teen, she craved the bonds between young women, and was able to create a handful of friendships among rogue teenage women, who were lasting friends to this day, who didn't care what others thought of them. These friends were all from different backgrounds. She believed she could relate to any other woman's experiences, regardless of their race, or color of their skin. She needed a girls' night out, badly.

Chapter Thirteen

            KATE
I need time with my friends.

            JOSH
What are you going to tell
them? About *us*?

            KATE
No.
       (She looks away)

I just haven't seen them
for awhile.

Josh sits on the sofa. He turns on the TV.

            KATE
So it's OK with you? I
know you wanted to
spend time with me.

            JOSH
I dunno, Kate. Sure. If it
makes you feel better.

Texting on her iPhone, Annie caught Christine at a free moment.

Artgal Annie: Hey Christine. How's life going in your world? Got to talk to you about this guy I was seeing.

Crazy Christine: Hey~ comin' to my place next week? To discuss what's been going on in our neck of the woods?

Artgal Annie: Yes! Looking forward! Much to bitch and moan about, my pal.

Crazy Christine: OMG the guy at the market, what an attitude. More later.

Artgal Annie: More men problems? You know we enjoy that part of life/Smiley face/No excuses about being too old for all of this! Paula might join us after her gig....

The summer sun shining through the bay windows of Christine's house warmed Annie, as she came through the door. Her rock garden was colorful, and displayed the good tastes of the woman that lived there perfectly. Annie put some of her groceries on the counter and joined her friend in her large living room. Someday I'm going to live in a house like this one, big and spacious, with my own desk and light table. With a guy who's the right one for me. Snap back from daydreaming.

"I'm walking down the street to get to work and some guy whistles at me," said Christine, her long blonde hair falling like a lion's mane past her shoulders. Annie's friend since high school days continued, "I tell him, *firmly,* 'Hey look, you do not whistle to women. I do not answer to a whistle. You're not the right type!" Just the way she said it made Annie laugh. You knew there was no messing with Christine. "Men have to learn. We will not settle as doormats for them.

"Yes," said Annie, decisively . She agreed to that. Another good female buddy, Paula, with her beautiful black skin setting off her large, almond eyes, planned on taking off some time off of her tour as a rock musician. Like Kay, she cared nothing for makeup and men's expectations of her. She balanced her travel with a good year-long contract to play with her band at a local nightclub in north Hollywood. A picture-perfect liberated woman.

Annie talked for days with them about Eastern and Western philosophy and the perks of getting drunk on beers. And speaking compassionately about how much trouble they caused their parents growing up during their teens.

"Good god, we watched that 8mm dirty movie you found thrown on the sidewalk near your childhood home. And your dad yelling, 'What nonsense are you up to?!' while we were locked inside your bedroom."

"I remember that well," Annie said, exhaling a breath and shaking her head. "Don't embarrass me!" she smiled, laughing, while Christine laughed out loud with a sigh.

Then Annie remembered what she and Ian had talked about before, about staying friends with each other. Ian didn't think of himself as being bad. She forgave him for not telling her about Piper.

"Oh! Before I forget!" Annie brought over some egg tarts she bought in Chinatown and Christine promptly poured out two glasses of Chardonnay for the two of them. They both hoped Paula could make it for her week off in L.A. between her band playing in Seattle and San Francisco. She would love to see some of her old friends.

Annie was eager to join them after all the hectic hours at work and just to be around other female friends. So she didn't have to bother feeling bad about any relationship problems. She was just out with the girls. In addition to the egg tarts, she brought a package of Crispy Donuts that she hugged close to her bright red coat.

"Hey, did I tell you about the guy who works at Super Saver Market? The one who thinks he's God's gift to women? Such a show-off!" Christine sputtered, in between tasting the egg tarts and wine. "I see him every time I shop at that grocery store," she sneered. "He thinks he's so great, flirting with the cashiers."

"Ha! You are so funny, Christy," laughed Annie, "I know the type, I've told you about all that," trying to keep her mind off of it, as Christine's record player blasted some '70's music that brought back old memories. She loved how Christine had a story to tell for just about anything going on in her life, and was able to laugh at it. As "We Are the Champions", the iconic song by Queen played, Annie offered her desserts. "Here, have another egg tart," Annie hastily said, as she laid out the dessert on the gold-trimmed plates that showed off Christine's impeccable taste in fine dinnerware, for her best female friend.

"I've got man trouble," Annie shared. "Those guys need to control themselves. If more than one girl gets interested in them, they start thinking they can have them all! I am officially not dating Bill the Bachelor!"

"Hurray to that one! You go girl!" shouted Christine, as she cheered her with her wine goblet. Annie and Christine sipped their drinks, feeling like they could say anything at all around each other. "Good for you. I bet you feel better that you graduated from that class real quick," said Christine, always present to support a friend.

The doorbell rang. "Must be Paula," Annie said, as she arched her neck forward and greeted a short, frumpy lady who she thought was Paula at first. She had a grimace on her face, looking insulted that Annie dared to call her anything but her given name.

"Is Christine there?" the lady insisted. It was Christine's upstairs neighbor, Mrs. Catty. "Yes. Is there a problem?" Annie asked.

"You can tell her she better turn that music down. My husband is trying to watch his football game and it's getting in the way to hear all that noise!"

Christine came to the door, obligingly. "Oh, is it the noise from my speakers? I'm sorry. I'll turn it down. I know what it's like trying to watch a show with loud music going on."

"It's just that he's always around the television, I can't get him to stop," Mrs. Catty confided, frowning, almost teary eyed.

Christine laughed. In 99% of her relations with others, she created happiness for them.

"I can't begin to tell you what I'm like with someone else's music blasting when I do my beadwork." All of her friends knew how devoted she was to her artwork in silver and gold needlework that she proudly displayed around her house. Next time if that happens and it's too loud just give me a call, here's my number," as she jotted her number down on a napkin.

But when she was out of earshot, Christine said to Annie, "That woman, if it's not the music, it's how her husband watches his games and TV every day, or how he doesn't help with the chores," as she rolled her eyes and described her neighbor in detail. "She complains he's out with his friends having a good time. You can't hold someone down like that. Always something around here, never a dull moment!" she laughed again, as Annie snickered.

They were going to launch into another tirade when Paula, with her reddish-brown hair and low, throaty voice, came smiling up to the open door. Annie was quick to stretch her arms out to embrace her friend, who travelled miles from New York City to play in North Hollywood and just spend a little time with her West Coast friends.

"I heard that, Christine~! And I will be sure to tell Mrs. Catty all about it," she joked. She brought along her guitar and sat on the couch, stretching her arms and legs. "Whoo, I needed that after that plane trip.

"Play us something, Paula," said Annie, and Christine followed up with, "Yeah, something you played on tour," She decided to comfort her two friends with a love ballad.

"Too bad that's not like real life, like my mom always said ..." Paula quipped. "My mother would spend hours on the couch watching old Hollywood romance movies and would lecture me on how far from the truth those love stories were. But I believe love can be that way, even better than the movies, sometimes."

"I feel exactly the same way!" Annie added.

"Like my Aubrey, I can tell her about anything and she'll listen. We've been through a lot. You know, with people finding out I came out of the closet. Aubrey was a lifesaver to me." Christine poured a glass of wine for her. She took a sip of Chardonnay. "All my fans. Half of them supported me, half of them deserted me. I would introduce Aubrey up on stage, and some of the fans in the audience would throw things at her. It was so humiliating for her. I couldn't believe the mindset of those monsters. But she saved me from what could have been hell for me.

It was her idea to have me play for the Hunger Charity and Up For LGBTQ festival this year right here in LA." Lesbian Paula was right. Love could be a lifesaving experience.

I feel exactly the same way with Ian. He saved me on the rebound from all those users. Who took advantage of me.

"I know how it feels when moms, dads and chums try to bring you down to earth. Like they tell you real life never has the guy tell you 'I love you', said Annie, feeling jaded again. "Well, I did have a guy say that to me …"

She stopped and paused for good on that one. She didn't want to go over her personal life now. Ian's advice spoke volumes to her now. Annie turned things around. Looking straight at Christine, she offered these words, "You know, you need to find someone you're really into, someone who you wouldn't mind taking you away. Yes, I think you need a vacation."

Christine got quiet for a few seconds, and softly agreed, "Yeah, maybe…." Christine's job as a waitress was a strain on her at times. "Or just by myself," her voice trailed.

"I meant with someone, a trustworthy friend, maybe," said Annie, assertively. "How's that guy, your friend Ted?"

"Oh he's fine…." Christine said, thoughtfully. "We're just getting to know each other better. This wine came from his vineyard in Lakeside." She paused, daydreaming, then came back to the present.

"Hey, let's have some of those donuts, we need a sugar high!" she shouted, and Annie couldn't agree more. Annie didn't want to bring up Ian to her friends. Not just now. It just wouldn't do to complain, or even to boast. She knew she had to make up her own mind about things. She felt strong enough to do that. So she just partied and enjoyed her female friends' company instead. She broke out the chocolate donuts and poured another cup of wine for all of the gals. A girl's night *in* this time. Worked like a charm, every time.

Chapter Fourteen

                    KATE
          I've had it up to here.
          You only care about your
          reputation. What about us?

                    JOSH
          Then maybe we better keep
          our distance and cool it
          on the relationship.

                    KATE
          You say that and then you
          regret it!

Back at work again after the party, she felt refreshed. That would last a few more hours, because she was intent on working on that script. It was soon after ten, then it was midnight. She kept typing on her computer. Annie's eyes were shut. She swayed and bent over and to the side, in her seat, trying to stay awake. She went to her fridge and brought out a six pack of Asian beer, and took out two bottles which she promptly chugged down. It tided her over while working on her script. Somehow she dragged herself to bed. She slept soundly and felt satisfied.

Soon it was morning and she woke up, made herself some breakfast, but cried as she tried to eat. She lost her appetite, but somehow managed to finish it. Dammit, this is what love is like? She wasn't in love with Ian, or was she?"

There was a ring on the phone, and she started getting a migraine as she massaged her temples and used acupressure to try to calm down. She scrambled around the room and found her cell phone, answering it promptly.

"Hey...I just thought I'd call and see how you're doing." It was Ian. "Oh no, are you crying?" he asked, as she sniffled. "I want you to be happy," he pleaded.

"I feel like going back to bed for the whole morning," she struggled to say. Ian was firm.

"That's the first sign of depression. Lie down and relax."

She felt better already. "O.K. I know I want to really win. I made it through my goal of eating my breakfast. That's not my only goal...I'm working on the final draft of my screenplay..."

"Just go back to sleep for awhile. You need to relax."

"O.K. Thank you so much for calling. Oh, and Ian? I wanted to add, thanks for talking to me. It helps me to win today and keeps me going."

The next week Annie pondered about this in her mind. Ian called and told Annie that *he* had made up his mind. He clearly had enough with the lady who rented him his room. Not enough privacy, he kept saying, with people over all the time. That's when Ian showed up outside the condo gate with several bags of his stuff. He looked like he was going to stay for awhile.

Plunking himself down on the sofa, he opened up to Annie. "Marissa was getting on my nerves. She wanted me out of there today. She already found a replacement tenant." That was quick, thought Annie.She put the fancy, frilly Ladies Secret underwear in her chest of drawers back into the box to send back for returns. No need to wear any of those. I'm not in a relationship now. She was still a little stunned that Dan had warned Ian so sternly about things. Maybe I should have kept my mouth shut about all this. I just couldn't keep it inside, she said to herself.

"OK, so this is our agreement. I stay until I find another place. I pay you rent money. We can still date. I just needed to get away," Ian explained. Annie obliged, it was only temporary, since she needed her small condo unit for herself. In the meantime, she liked his company. He was charming and fun to be around. She called him, "Boo Baby" and to him she was, "Pumpkin Head."

They hugged each other almost every hour. She never felt a friendship so trustworthy, so fulfilling.

She would set things right about Ian and Dan, no matter what Ian thought. It just wasn't fair. So she decided on it, finally. She was going to set the record straight on Ian. Tomorrow was a Friday at work, and she talked to Dan at Penchant, as he finished speaking with the production assistants about the first filming day taking place in Carmel.

He was rounding the corner in the hallway when she said without hesitation, "Dan? I heard you talked to Ian. About me and Ian…I want to say, please don't be hard on him. He's a good person. I think he should be allowed to stop by the company again." Dan rubbed his face, and then said without hesitation,

"O.K. No harm intended." He crossed and uncrossed his arms, thinking it over.

Annie persisted. "I mean, Ian has done a lot for both companies and for the merger. Think of that, Dan." She hoped she wasn't overstepping her boundaries, but she had to let him know. Dan was mostly a quiet man, who believed in the potential of everyday people.

"I was just trying to protect you, Annie. In general, we don't want there to be conflict with our staff and any outside employees." He changed gears and said, "You are a talented artist and writer. Gayle told me about your writing. I wish you well with that."

Her spirits rose. She always appreciated other's comments about her work. "I was thinking, our daughter Allie is getting interested in writing screenplays," he said, rubbing the stubble on his chin. "If you have any pointers to share with her on how to get started writing, let me know. You could talk to her about what's involved in the field and how you got into it. I think it would help her a lot."

"I'd love to, I'd be more than happy to help out," she said, and was more than enthusiastic to share experiences with her. A former shy girl coaching a younger shy girl. She was relieved and smiled.

He finally uncrossed his arms. "I'll have Allie give you a call so you can offer advice on how to write her first screenplay. You can be a mentor to her. And I intend on paying you for this, too, Annie." The prospect of her, Annie, mentoring another person in the sometimes daunting task of screenwriting gave Annie the impetus to keep writing and believing in herself.

"Aww, that's sweet. We could even start next week, if that's OK with Allie." She looked forward to helping Allie break out of the mold and do something that pushed the envelope a bit. "Dan, she could even have the makings of a truly original screenwriter, with practice and hard work. Don't forget to mention it will be hard work. But I'm more than overjoyed to mentor a young woman."

"Great! We'll start next week. I'm also looking forward to her bright future. You know, she's been hanging around a bad crowd, a bad influence. I think she would appreciate you helping with her studies."

"No worries, always happy to help." She smiled, confident she was doing the right thing. "You know, I was like her, going through that phase. Being a young adult can be a confusing thing. I know. I'm kind of glad I got beyond that," she chuckled softly.

"Me included, Annie, me included," said Dan, his mellow side taking over again.

Chapter Fifteen

KATE
They've asked me to mentor
their daughter. Truth is,
I've never done this before.
I don't know if I've got it
in me to do this. I've got
to get ready for this.

JOSH
Well, you're a writer. Just
talk like one writer to
another.

KATE
What if she gets bored?
Or starts getting an
attitude towards me?

JOSH
Just treat her like any
other. You were a young
adult once.

The following week, she scheduled time to get together with Allie. Over the phone, when she called Annie, she seemed a little shy at first, but Annie could tell she really wanted to connect. "Meet me in my office. We'll go over the details later," Annie said, while Allie headed over almost right away. She's very eager, that's a good sign.

"So where to, Allie? Did you want me to pick you up tomorrow before work and go to a nearby café? A coffee shop is a great place to brainstorm with a laptop, or simply take notes on the strangers around you. It sometimes makes for great dialogue, when your descriptions start to get too cliché and boring."

Looking at Allie, Annie was reminded of how she was at that age. It was a great age to start out as an artist or writer, hormones raging and all. And those mood swings could really help her be more creative.

"Would you like me to pick you up and go to Earth café? It's a ten-minute drive from here." Allie seemed excited to get started. Dressed in black, again, but this time she wore a bright pink scarf around her waist that seemed to signify her interest in turning bright ideas into interesting stories. They could smell the rich brews of espresso and café lattes when they entered the cozy café. Annie wanted to break the ice with her.

"So what kind of music do you like?" She wasn't sure if she was trying to act younger to relate well to the Gen Z young woman. She herself felt a little awkward.

Allie smiled, and thought for a minute. "Umm, I like post-punk, some rap, alternative rock…tone, and style." She paused. A bit awkwardly.

Annie focused on what Allie was really there for. "How far are you in this screenplay of yours? Are you attending classes?"

"I'm taking English lit, and screenwriting. At UCLA."

"Good choice! How do you like the classes?"

"They're good," she said, lowering her gaze. She seemed to be hiding something. Annie tried to forget, too, her own feelings of envy.

"I just took a bootcamp class," Allie said, a little hesitantly. Annie gave herself a pinch in her thigh and reminded herself how important it was to mentor Allie. As a teen, Annie wished she had someone to guide her.

"Have you written an outline? I find it helps to do that, so you can more easily change the characters and plot if you feel you have to do that. Did they cover that in your course at all?"

"The teacher told us to start with an idea and a beginning, middle, and an end to our screenplay." OK, she seems to have gotten that together.

"Then you're wondering where to begin, how to get inspiration for a script?" Allie smiled at this, looking a bit over Annie's shoulder.

"Kind of…" she said, shyly.

"What genre are you going to write in, for this screenplay of yours? A little shy again, but more confidently, she replied, "I like horror movies. I think I'd like to write a screenplay in the thriller and horror genre."

Oh no, Annie thought, quickly. Horror movies were not up her alley. Maybe thrillers, but she couldn't stand the blood. Unlike her mother, the doctor, who probably looked at dead people during her stay as a resident in a local hospital. "Oh, good choice!" she remarked, eager to inspire the young woman. "Horror movies are a very popular genre. They make a lot of them in Hollywood, or anywhere a low-budget movie can be made. You could collaborate with a small, independent film company or director and go from there. They can be made on a modest budget, too."

She noticed Allie smile more, though still looking down and off to the side. Annie continued, "Sometimes going out for walks, or exercising, doing other active things can be time spent finding inspiration," hoping that she wasn't boring Allie.

"What else are you doing besides screenwriting and literature classes?" Maybe that was an intrusion, but she really wanted to help.

"I'm taking electric guitar lessons," she smiled, opening up more.

"Electric guitar classes!" She wasn't expecting that. "Are you enjoying that?"

Allie smiled and acknowledged with a nod. "I think it helps me express myself. It's a little like writing. It's creative."

"Wonderful. You are so talented."

"I like to do creative things. I hope I can make a living

combining all of that."

"You could even get inspired from your own experiences, maybe a character works out or builds strength by her talents in your story."

She took this in, with a slight smile.

"And just keep on watching movies, see how the action is paced, when things are slow and when they are faster." She stopped and waited to hear her response.

"The thing is, I keep thinking an idea is going to be too silly or not worth a full-length screenplay. It's hard sometimes."

"Well, just allow yourself to write ideas down when they come in your head. You can pick and choose later which are the ones that can be developed." Even Annie was feeling more confident supporting Allie. Annie knew she was going to do well. She could see by the young women's sincerity.

"I just don't know if I have time for all my homework. I'm also working part-time at the bike shop on campus."

"You do this for extra money?"

"Yeah, and also to support other bike riders. Better for the environment and easy to get around campus."   She felt that Allie was opening up and believing in herself more.

"Would you like to meet again next time maybe, next month would be alright?"

She nodded.

"OK, Allie we'll meet again."

Chapter Sixteen

The next week Annie made preparations to start work on "Take Me Away", the last production for Penchant, so she packed an extra suitcase with the script revision copies for the cast, call sheets of production schedules and other reports to keep track of that day's shoot. Some of the others brought hard drives along with them to save all of the dailies for the directors to review.

Dragging the luggage along, to the condo exterior, she called Ian to remind him to fill his gas tank to full and they started on the four hour drive to Carmel after he picked up Annie. The plan was while she was working with the crew, he would visit some art galleries, and try to show her extensive work in painting to the art gallery owners, as her agent. He called beforehand to make the appointments.

It was going to be a relaxing time after work, she told herself.

He was her friend now, who decided he would spend some vacation time there with her. A work/vacation time. She hadn't had a real vacation in three years. "I'm getting to being married to my work. Which is not what I plan on doing from now on," she said, decisively. "Work is work, but you have to play sometimes," she said, and Ian couldn't agree more.

"I have bags under my eyes from all of the legal work I had to deal with concerning the merger," he confided. "Most of my clients were mad at each other about the transition. I spent hours trying to convince them that the move was the smartest decision they could make, that would allow their finances and human resources to become more accessible to each other." He stretched his arm outside of the window. "In other words, everyone from those two companies would be sharing job descriptions instead of overloading their own work duties. To put it bluntly, 'You don't have to be crazy to work for this company, we will train you."

Annie stretched her own arm out to release her tension, touching Ian's arm. She slid her hand on top of his, as if to calm him. Dropping her off at the location for the shoot, he gave her a hug. "Call me on your cell when you're done for the day. I'll let you know how it goes."

After arriving early, she met the cast and crew on the beach, who staked a colorful banner to show where they were located. She distributed the script revisions to the cast members, and made sure the directors and their assistants knew what scenes they were shooting that day. They were to film right on the beach in Carmel-by-the-Sea, and they couldn't have picked a better day. The sun made the waves sparkle with light. Cast and crew, above-the-line directors and assistants all went barefoot, with their loose light clothing waving like flags in the refreshing light wind.

"Sam, make sure that camera is at eye-level, no more of those crazy angles," Charlie reminded the assistant cameraman, "…and we need more of that reflected light," the DP called out to the women holding onto the large convex reflectors of silvery glass. "Actors, get on your marks and practice that run-through. Make sure you remember the blocking in this first shot."

After several minutes waiting for the actors' prep, the director called out to the cinematographers and sound people, "Speed, Roll Sound," and waited for the sound recordist to run for a few seconds, when he called out, "Sound Rolling," and Charlie called out, "Action," as the actors moved into position and began their dialogue.

Annie called out instructions to the background actors between takes and reminded them to pay attention to their blocking positions. Gayle commanded the actors and actresses with missed revisions or any straying from the lines they said. The two actors, the young woman with long dark hair and the male lead with equally dark locks hooked their eyes to each other. They both looked like a perfect couple with their suntanned skin and poreless facial features.

"Stay in that position," Charlie motioned for the two leads to pause. "No, darling, not with that expression. You're in love, remember? Come on, I want to see more *expression*," he waved his hands in the air, "Yes, that's right, get *closer,* get *closer,*" don't be shy..." You could see their grimaces after each take. The leading man and leading lady were obviously not chums with each other in real life. She kept grinning with her teeth tightly clenched.

"Charles, I can't do this," she rolled her eyes and started to have a meltdown.

The director had to have a word with her. "Angie, darling, you're doing fine. Just smile like you are falling in love," to which she sighed and put on a movie star grin.

"And get my good side, my part needs to look straight," she murmured to the hair stylist. Meantime, the leading man was having issues.

"I've been through this before," he frowned at Charles, taking him aside for a little private chat. "I can't stand it when she's like this," he whispered.

"Just try to keep it together. The audience really loved you in the last one together, Steve, you can do it again," Charles whispered back.

"Such a prima donna," he muttered, as she primped her hair and the hair and makeup artists did their final retouch ups on her.

Out of the corner of her eye, Annie saw trouble coming. A pair of preteen boys and another pair of girls were laughing and playing with their water buckets. As they came into view in the lens of the cinematographer, one of them tripped over themselves and a bucket of water splashed right over the two stars, leaving Angie a screaming mess and Steve in shock, shaking his hair to remove all the mess of sand and sea from his face.

"Oh good god!" yelled Charles. Gesturing wildly to the crew, he said, "OK hair and makeup, those extra towels will come in handy for this one!" as they immediately pulled out extra beach towels to dry off the two stars. Annie tried hard to keep a laugh from erupting inside, but failed at this miserably.

While the actors and actresses did several takes, it took the patience of a good director to try to bring the best out of them. Camera angles were challenging and the crew worked hard to keep their equipment steady with sandbags and sealed equipment to keep out the ocean's moisture and sand. After thoroughly catching as much of the action on film as they could, the crew finally disbanded after eight hours of intense work. before they called it a day.

"I'm done, for the day, Ian," she said on her cell. She couldn't wait to see him, and how he did speaking with the gallery owners.

"How was your day?" he smiled. "Crazy," was her response. He opened her palms and put some business cards he picked up from three gallery owners into them. "They seemed interested in your work. Now you've got to contact them, my work on that is done." She tried to resist the urge to kiss him.

It was an opportunity that Ian and Annie took, as the others packed up their equipment and actors' assistants left with the crew and directors, to stay behind and walk to the nearest café to get drinks and pastries and share it between themselves on the beach. Annie took out a folded beach blanket from her straw tote bag to spread out over the beaches' soft warm sand, and they happily treated themselves to the pastries and warm croissants, washing it down eagerly with pink lemonade.

"I really love being in this business," Annie smiled at Ian, sitting closer to him on the warm blanket, that soaked in the late afternoon's sunrays. "I mean, even though there's bound to be clashes, and sometimes even chauvinistic macho males and divas, it is so creative to collaborate on something that can turn out to be something you're proud of. There are a lot of strong women in the history of filmmaking. And there is so much talent, too. Me, I like to put words in people's mouths. It's crazy, but it can be really powerful, too."

Before she could outdo him in her enthusiasm for work, Ian said, "That's why I want to be an entertainment lawyer. I'm learning about the business everyday. I like to represent actors because they are so creative...some of the director's can infringe on their basic rights, you know, with all the philandering going on in Hollywood. I guess I would be out of work if it wasn't for those types, though...."

He turned to gaze at Annie's eyes, and put his arm around her shoulder. "Looks like the sun is cooperating here," he said, as he pointed at the amazing sunset. They turned to watch shades of bright neon orange light up the sky. A yellow streak where the sun started to disappear complemented the purple water reflecting off of the heavens. He looked again into her eyes, a smile forming on his face, then a look of wonder.

"Ian, do you believe in love? I mean, when two people really feel something. Like warmth and security?" He smiled but the two busted out laughing. Getting corny again, she thought. He brushed her hair off of her forehead and kissed her on the lips, then they hugged each other for what seemed like an eternity. He wanted it that way, and so did she.

He stood up, shaking out his cargo pants clad legs. "Let's take a walk around the water, and go along Pebble Beach," he said. "You need the fresh air and I would love the workout," he smiled.

"OK, I'm on to it!" beamed Annie, as she pushed herself up from the sand. Ian took her hand and they walked together, side by side, their toes getting a bit of therapy walking in the warm, wet sand. They both felt like they were ten years younger, shoulders brushing each other and the two of them making up the whole world.

"We'll check out the local cuisine," she added, already working up her appetite. When they reached their hike of one mile after thirty minutes, they shook out their sand-filled sandals and headed to downtown Carmel, where they spotted Jerry's Place, with their menu turning out to be a simple but fresh place to get hot hoagie sandwiches and a mug of beer. She could drink occasionally, she said to herself. And not by herself. They sat at the counter bar, and they lifted their mugs in celebration.

"It's officially the end of the shoot here!" as they clinked their glasses and took big sips of the gourmet brew. The place was rockin', with a good, danceable cover band playing, and the exposure to the sun made her face resonate with a healthy glow. The deep brown skin of the classy, sexy lead singer added to the sultriness of the moment, as she belted out, "Then Came You," by the Spinners and featuring Dionne Warwick. Annie was taken back to when she was in middle school, listening to this iconic hit from the seventies on her family's old transistor radio.

She stood up and pulled on Ian's arm, who tried to resist, "I don't dance…" but she managed to get him to freestyle move to the irresistible music. About thirty minutes dancing to the retro music, Ian sputtered, "OK, OK, I know I'm really out of shape…" he breathed heavily, "so…so I will have to decline any more dance requests…at least for now," he chuckled.

"We should definitely do this more often," she said in his ear. "It's a great workout and my tummy needs to get in shape," she said with a magnetic look in her brown eyes and a wry smile. The DJ perfectly blended in the falsetto voices of the Stylistics as "You Make Me Feel Brand New" filled the air, and Annie stepped over Ian's shoes as they got close, stomachs touching and the passion flowing. She chuckled to herself, remembering this song from years ago. "Could It Be I'm Falling in Love" reached their ears even as they left the restaurant. They became so lost in their heartfelt feelings for each other that reality was starting to get harsh.

She knew, on the drive home, that she would only have a limited time with Ian before he moved back to Huntington Beach to rejoin Piper, so she savored every moment with Ian as much as she could. With his playlist blasting, Ian and Annie had their own karaoke party singing to "Mirror in the Bathroom" along the highway home.

In a few days, Annie unexpectantly got a visit from Ian. He called on his cell and she went to see him at the gate. For a few seconds she looked at him through the rails of the gate and felt the distance between them. She opened the metal door and walked up to him closely near the sidewalk, sensed something would be shifting in their friendship, but she didn't really want to face it.

She quickly opened the pedestrian gate and stood outside with Ian.

Hands jammed into his black jeans, he announced, "I'm going back to Huntington Beach. I'm gonna move back in with Piper." She could see it took a lot of courage for him to say this.

She took in a breath and held it as he continued. "Then we'll be married." She almost moved in for a kiss, then drew back at the news. "No. It's not a good cause." She was genuinely hurt by all of this. He impatiently responded, "I don't want to think about tomorrow. I just want to enjoy now!"

"You said you'd marry Piper," she insisted he realize this.

"Piper's not here! Piper and I are not married! She's miles away from here." He tried to kiss her but she pulled away.

"What? This is just cuddling…"

She moved away from him. "Ian, we'll be friends. Just good friends. I don't want to hurt you, but it's for the best. I mean, you've got somebody who loves you already. I'm setting you free. And forgive me for ordering you to leave her. I know it was wrong."

"You've been talking to your friends."

"No, I realized it for myself. I need my own life back. Go call Piper now. Be with her. What's holding you back?"

He crossed his arms, then uncrossed them, putting a thumb on her face to stroke her cheek. "I guess it's because I always wanted to meet someone like you. Someone who is creative and beautiful. I love everything about you."

Suddenly shivering in the cool weather, wearing only a beach coverup over her shorts and T-shirt, she was not letting her mind waver. She stamped her feet back and forth to keep warm, sandals brushing the sand still lingering from the beach in Carmel between her toes, and said, "We'll be friends, always. Now go do what you gotta do." She almost wanted him to rub her arms to warm her up.

"O.K. I understand. "And Annie?" He waited until she turned to him again. "I want you to do a painting. Of McGregor, my cat. It's for Piper."

"A present? You're giving it to her? But he's *your* cat," she said, a bit confused. "Yup. It's a secret," he replied.

Decisively, she said, "You're going to see your cat, Ian. And you'll be seeing your family. Enjoy yourself."

Turning on her heels, she clutched at the grate of the metal door, used her fob key, and opened the door for herself, sighing as she reached her place.

Chapter Seventeen

                    KATE
          Is it because of Trudy??

                    JOSH(sighing)
          Kate, we went over this.

                    KATE
          Josh, it's time you
          decided.

                    JOSH
          I don't want to talk
          about it.

                    KATE
          OK, we'll work this out.
          I believe we can.

Ian leaned against the murals next to the tiled wall with a Hollywood theme, sitting in the subway train waiting area. He was eager to see his family again, especially his dad. They always got along great, and recently he was concerned about Ian's welfare, mostly his love life. There was something about Piper he was never able to convince his father about. "What's that girlfriend of yours trying to make you do now?" his dad had asked Ian.

Ian stepped up to defend her. "I had the great good fortune of meeting her." Piper really did look good for her fifty plus age, with a flat stomach she got through working out at the gym. After a half hour drive thinking this over, he told himself that all of Piper's demands were only her nervous emotions before their marriage, and that they would all dissolve like smoke after they finally got hitched.

He arrived at their apartment around seven at night, exhausted and looking forward to meeting Piper for dinner. Piper was looking good and dressed nicer than usual, in a flowing red dress.

"Hey!" he said as he asked, "So where do you want to go for dinner?" he asked, going to the bedroom and riffling through the clothing in their closet. "Where's that shirt and tie I put aside? I remember I put it in one spot for special occasions. This is weird. I remember I put it there before I left. And there's a pair of slacks missing," he said, suspiciously. "Where's all my video games? I put them right here in this box!" he pointed in the closet. Did you move them?"

"You'll find them," she said, offhandedly. She changed her tone. It was suddenly very pointed. "Maybe it's because you have too much stuff. It gets piled up all the time. You really should be spending money on me instead of on yourself," she demanded, placing her hands on her hips. "What about *me* for a change?" She put on a jealousy act to cover up her theft. It was certain there was someone she was giving gifts to on the side. And some things that belonged to Ian.

When he asked once again about dinner, she replied, "Oh, Ian...I am so sorry," almost sarcastically. "I completely forgot. I already had dinner with a friend...and I had to pick you up, I was so hungry. You understand..."

Ian threw up his hands and slammed his head back. "Piper, we planned on this!" he reacted, disappointed. Then, still being suspicious, he asked, "So who was this person you had dinner with?" It was clear Piper tried to cover this up.

"Oh, just a friend. Someone from work," she lied. "Ian, it's just a little thing. You are way too sensitive. I've got leftovers from last night I can warm up for you. Your favorite, lasagna!"

"But you said we would have a nice dinner together .... I've missed you, and my family..."

"Ian, it was just a little thing. Are you sure you don't want to finish the leftovers?"

He sighed, took out his phone from his jacket, and ordered Chinese takeout instead. And even then, there was no avoiding her demands.

He winced as she demanded, "And Ian, order me some egg rolls. I want two orders. Don't forget the dipping sauce. And the sweet and sour pork. And a Pepsi, too as long as you're there."

He didn't want to, he was tired from his trip. But he did so anyway, to appease her. If he didn't, he knew what he was in for. Last time when he wanted to watch a movie she didn't like, she threw a tantrum and more.

"You only think of yourself," she had said. Don't you know we're in a relationship? You should be putting me on a pedestal but instead you are being so selfish. And just the other day. All I asked is if you could buy me that dress I was looking at last time I shopped at the store. You promised it as my birthday present. My *late* birthday present, by the way!"

He still considered himself fortunate he had her as a girlfriend, she was pretty, after all. He never had that female attention in high school. They met through other friends who introduced them. But instead of being grateful to them, and to Ian, she shouted, "I've told Chelsea and Matthew how selfish and controlling you are, I had to, you were being too much for me to handle!" she complained.

She flew into these rages and accused him of doing things he never did, and he ended up always trying to placate her when she was angry at him. Once they were shopping at a department store together for cheap plastic furniture they needed when they had just moved in together. He remembered Piper saying out loud at the store, "Ian, you were looking at that girl, didn't you? Why were you staring at her? Maybe we need time apart, you have your eyes on other things….," not bothering to lower her voice in front of the other shoppers. And, "I'll talk to your mother about the way you talked to me. She'll set things straight!" including other ridiculous assumptions just to control him.

They were together seven years. It was almost as if he was used to being treated that way. Maybe it was best we stayed apart for awhile, until my work stabilized and I passed the bar, he ruminated. I bet things will change once I become an established lawyer. Absence does make the heart grow fonder.

He knew Annie wanted to cool it with him for this reason, and he imagined what it might feel like if Piper ever confronted Annie about their friendship. That must have been why Annie kept breaking up with him. Although he guessed she never really had him in the first place.

Annie needed a change. She needed more freedom to rethink her friendship with Ian, and even better, she said to herself, to forget about him. "I'm going to try online dating," she told him, over the phone. She didn't feel the need to be secretive about this to her friend.

"Annie," he sighed, rolling his eyes heavenward. "Don't just go out with the first guy you meet," he warned her.

Chapter Eighteen

                KATE
        I just thought, maybe I
        better start dating again.
        I mean, I don't want to
        cheat over your girlfriend.
        We're just friends now,
        you know.

                JOSH
        OK, OK. I get it. But I
        get first dibs on you.

The next morning, Annie got in front of her computer and looked up the reactions to her dating profile she had listed online. She wanted to look nice, so she spent a lot of money on headshots by a photographer who as one of her neighbors in the condo she lived in. She was broke now. Well, it couldn't hurt, I could always use them, too, for resume photos to find work or for online profiles on places like facebook. She looked at a few photos of guys online, some of them looking like prospects, some who never answered back.

Overall not very exciting to her, except one guy who left a message that he wanted to meet in person. She completely ignored Ian's advice he said earlier, about not going out with the first guy she met. "Hi Harry. I'll take you up on that. Lunch sounds good to me. Call me." Wonder how this will turn out, she thought, just coming out of the shower.

The phone rang. She wrapped herself in a pink cheetah robe. "Hi, Harry! How are you? You still wanna meet for Chinese food?"

She nodded to herself. "I'd love to go window shopping with you," she said, happy to have a date. So who was desperate now? She didn't want to appear that way. "At the Grove in L.A."

The photo in his profile was a picture of a young Japanese-American man, in a white, starched shirt and tie. Annie later found out he was a used car salesman. He was attractive, and Annie wanted to find out more about him. He agreed to Annie's idea to meet at the mall. They met in front of a gift store in the outdoor area.

He was sitting, waiting for her, his back a bit hunched over. Not too cheerful of a guy, she thought. He didn't even say hi or smile. That was her first impression. "Harry!" Harry averted her greeting. Like he had waited for hours for her. Even though it was really only five minutes. We'll see how it goes, she said to herself. He's not too talkative now.

It was a busy place that day at the mall, where crowds of young people walked around, young women wearing the latest styles, striped black and white skin tight leggings and short shorts with over the knee high boots.

Annie wore a tight miniskirt with a tight top. She tried to ignore the pain in her bunion while almost tripping on the slides that offered no support for a forty-plus year old woman. Annie's eyes focused on Harry, as they walked along. Then she noticed her favorite clothing store. It was the ever popular "Ladies Secret" lingerie boutique.

"Oh, wait a minute. Do you mind if I go in here for awhile? Just checking out the clothing", she said as she pointed to the lingerie store. Harry averted his eyes. "No, it's fine."

He waited on a bench that seemed strategically placed facing the store. She walked in and started to look at every single bra, from pink ruffly numbers, cream and black bras and lacy panties to match, in neat little drawers for the different sizes.

After maybe half an hour going throughout the entire store, she finally chose a black and pink bra with a black bow, and a cream-colored bra with ruffles and went to the dressing room in back. Oh no, I just finished taking a hoarding class. What the hell am I doing?

A saleswoman approached her near the dressing rooms and asked her if she needed any help. "What do you think about this one?" asked Annie, trying on the pink ruffled bra.

"I like it. It's playful. Whose it for?"

"Just someone I'm dating."

As if the saleswoman was psychic, or was just simply experienced in the game, she said, "Give it two weeks to get serious. After that the relationship should be called off."

In a few minutes, Annie walked out. Oblivious to others, she came out wearing only the ruffled bra and her panties, like nothing was wrong. She continued to look at some lingerie, until the saleslady noticed her. "Oh, look! There's a woman walking around in nothing but panties and a bra!" she shouted to her co-worker. Annie woke up from her dream world, and stopped, suddenly aware of what was happening.

She stared in shock at what little she had on. "I'm sorry! Oh, my god, what am I doing?" She ran back into the dressing room and left in her street clothes. "I didn't realize what I was doing! You must think I'm crazy!" Annie left the store in a hurry, embarrassed at her lack of discreetness. She didn't have the money for the boutique stores, only the online clothing sales.

Harry had waited for her for over half an hour. Obviously, he was not too thrilled. Rolling his eyes, with no eye contact whatsoever, he got up off the bench. "Sorry it took so long! I got in a little trouble while trying on some bras." They stopped into a skin care store she wanted to look through. He took liberties and started to flirt with the saleswoman. Don't know what they were talking about, she thought. Well, maybe he's just the friendly type.

They decided on dinner at Wong's restaurant, the cement horses standing guard outside the restaurant signaling that the restaurant was a more classy dining experience than her usual takeout dinners. It turned out the takeout food was better than the over-priced unauthentic Chinese lunch in a polished setting.

After they launched into the meal, Harry recounted his experiences with his ex-wife. "She once sent me a Valentine's Day card right before our divorce. It hinted that she had done something to my car. I look over at it in the driveway and she had spray painted all over the outside of it. She had it in her to stoop so low. And she started dating someone before we divorced." He grimaced, thinking about it.

"Oh, that's terrible!" Annie said, out of sympathy. "I don't know anyone like that. I've been too busy writing my screenplays. They're romantic comedies," she said, with pride. Harry shot back. "I watched a romantic comedy the other night. After that, I had to watch five football movies just to get over watching that one chick flick."

Sticking up for herself, she explained, "In my screenplay a woman has to choose between two men. And eventually, between the two, she finds the right one.

Harry said, stoically, "Why don't you write it so the woman ends up with the wrong guy? See how that turns out."

"The wrong guy?" She was dumbfounded. For about five seconds she had a brief idea of how that story might work in her screenplay. Fortunately it was only five seconds, because she sure as hell wasn't going to change it after the five second opinion of a stranger.

As he drove her home, he launched into a boring tirade of life as a used car salesman, and she didn't really think they had much in common to talk about. When they reached her place, he gave her a box of Chinese pastries, and Annie noticed later that one of them was eaten already. After a week or two Annie called back again, and Harry promised, "I *will* call you."

But of course, he never did. She should have known better than have him wait while she tried out bras. But the way he avoided eye contact. Forget it Annie, she thought. He was a bore. She got on the computer again. Relentless.

Chapter Nineteen

                KATE
    I started internet dating.
            (pauses)
    But so far, not much luck.

                JOSH
    Kate, are you getting
    intimate with these guys?
    You gotta give yourself
    room for a friendship
    first. Are you sleeping
    with any of these guys?

                KATE

    No, no….

            (sighing)

    I wouldn't do that with
    someone I don't like.
    Or someone with no
    chemistry between us.

She was on three dating sites this time. This was on dating site number 2. Hmmm, she thought. 37 years old. Bobby. A nice Chinese guy. Why not? They exchanged numbers and before she knew it, they both were curious to meet.

"Hi, Bobby? I was interested in your profile. What do you do?"

"I work as a weight loss training course teacher. At Bold's gym." "Cool! I'm a screenwriter," Annie replied, "I'm looking forward to meeting you, too. Yeah, I like Chinese food. Yeah." She nodded her head. "Hey, do you mind me asking?" Annie said, firmly. Did you ever want to have kids with someone, someday?"

"Yeah! When do we start?" She could see the humor in this, and she liked him immediately for this. Over lunch, he told her he was a part-time actor who got a part in a famous Chinese movie, "Memoirs of a Hooker, in the final scene as a fisherman. Annie found that to be interesting. They soon took off for the Santa Monica Music Festival. After an afternoon of salsa dancing performances, where Bobby whooped and awkwardly shook his booty to the music, Annie waited with him at the bus stop to go home.

"Hey that was fun, Bobby. I really enjoyed myself. It was nice meeting you." She thought he was nice, but not really her type. No sparks flew, anyway. When his bus arrived, he gave a wet, sloppy kiss on the cheek to Annie. Just the kind of kiss she couldn't stand.

OK. Dating site number 3.

Someone answered her email. Annie, excited at the prospect of another date, with a male nurse who worked at a hospital in L.A., she stayed up late talking to him over the phone. Annoyed, he tried to tell her he had to go to work early in the morning. The next day, after stepping out from the shower, her cell phone rang. Coyly, she answered, gushing, "You caught me at the right time. I was in my birthday clothes. Just out of the shower ..."

It was a lame attempt to sound sexy on her part.

Until he explained to her he was going to go back and date another woman he knew from before..because...he claimed he was "on.the same page" as she was..."You seem like a good person, you should be able to find someone else," he said, as Annie felt the false pity coming out of him. She hated false pity. Grrr.

She wasn't getting anywhere with online dating. She looked at her phone. Jim was again already one of the top people to call. Great. Something to look forward to. Her newfound optimism was paying off. She brushed her hair in the mirror. This will be fun, she thought. And Jim *is* a nice guy. So she planned to have dinner with him the next night.

That next night, before she could make a call to remind him, her cell phone went off. Jim was on his phone among the clutter surrounding him. Papers were on the couch, clothes were in three-foot piles, books scattered on the floor, bottles of men's perfume on the bathroom counter.

"Hello?" she answered. "Oh, hi, Annie, this is Jim." He sounded nervous, especially on the 'Oh, hi', part.

Annie sensed something was wrong. "Yeah, hi…Jim?" His voice, scattered, said, "Um, could we get together next Tuesday, instead? I'm cleaning out my house. You know, getting rid of clutter and cleaning up." He added, brightly, "You're a good influence on me."

"Alright," she said, disappointed. She got off the phone. Immediately after this, her phone rang again. "Yeah, hi Jim." What now? thought Annie.

"Listen, I got this coupon to eat out at my favorite restaurant. You would love it. But I want to use it tonight by myself. Let's get together next Friday, instead. I'm still cleaning out my house. I lost all this weight. You won't recognize me." Not again, she thought to herself, quickly. "Alright," she said, reluctantly. She hadn't even noticed if he was overweight or not.

When she relayed this to Ian, he gave his opinion on this.

"If it were me, I wouldn't wait a single minute." Annie thought, that's what I like about Ian. There wasn't any passion at all between her and Jim. He seemed awfully selfish using the coupon on his own dinner by himself. He lost a lot of points in Annie's mind and it was definitely a red flag for her. But since she told him she would get together, she made up her mind about it.

Friday night came after a slow week at work. It's OK, I got to work more on my screenplay, she said to herself. The next week she found herself talking to Jim again. "Meet me at the station in an hour," she said, and got him to agree to that. She primped herself in the mirror and put on lipstick.

This would be a good opportunity to take care of this, she thought as she pulled out the pair of electric blue high heels she tried to wear but still couldn't walk in them. And there was no shame in doing this for Annie. Wearing a pair of walking sneakers instead, she headed towards the local train station. Autumn was in the air and it was already freezing cold near the ticket booths, later in the evening around seven.

Annie was wearing her secondhand leather pants. "Where *is* he?" she said, almost out loud, half an hour later. She adjusted her sweater, then unzipped her pants to tuck her shirt in, hoping no one was watching her. In the process of doing this, the zipper got stuck and broke. "Damn!" she swore under her breath. She rubbed her shoulders to fend off the windy weather. In another hour and a half, Jim finally made it to the station. He didn't make eye contact. No sign of remorse for being over an hour late.

"It's freezing!" she said, as he sauntered over towards her as if nothing was amiss. And his hair! What did he do to his hair? Instead of raking it over his bald head, which was bad enough, his light brown frizzy hair stuck up on either side of his head, near his ears that resembled built-in ear muffs. Only it wasn't snowing.

No attraction to him, whatsoever. She was just passing time at this point. It seemed obvious that he was just going through the motions himself. "What took you so long!" Annie knew she might come across as being mean to him. But she *was* freezing, and he *was* over an hour and a half late.

After getting into his car, she pulled out the pair of high heels.

"Oh, before I forget. Here. Here's the shoes you bought for me. I really can't wear them, they hurt my feet bad! And my back. But thanks for thinking about me." His expression suddenly melted as he stared at the blue stilettos.

"Ohhh. But they're so nice! Maybe you could keep them. And look at them in your closet." At that moment she noticed he had several teeth missing that she hadn't noticed before. Except for the two buck teeth. She suddenly thought he resembled a rabbit.

"No, I'm not gonna do that," she said, stubbornly, about the blue heels. Then she noticed he had a Frieda's of Hollywood catalog on the floor of his car near her feet. "You can look at that catalog if you want," he said, trying to be amiable. "There might be something you like or look good in, yeah, yeah. That's great…"

"No, thanks, it's not my style," she said, immediately. She glanced at the models wearing black lace undergarments that barely covered their bodies." OK, I set that straight. She was turned off that he was trying to fit her in that sex diva role. She didn't think they were sexy, or anything like what she would ever wear.

On the way over to the restaurant, Jim reached into his shoulder bag.

"Oh, I forgot….," he said as he searched all throughout the bag, spilling some stray change and tissues onto his car seat and the interior of his floor. "I can't find that coupon. It said it would be good at any restaurant near the mall." Wow, he's pretty cheap, thought Annie, and she swore to herself she'd rather not be a cheapskate to anyone else she knew, knowing how she felt at that moment.

At Szechuan Villa, an upscale Chinese restaurant specializing in gourmet spicy hot fare, they ate hot pickled cabbage. Trying to keep her spirits up, she smiled at Jim.

"Good, huh?" she asked. Jim seemed a little distracted. "Yeah, yeah, it's really good..." She could tell he was just trying to be polite.

"Try the fish soup with hot peppers on top." Beautiful bright red peppers were scattered on top of the succulent fish soup. Jim suddenly got stuck in a coughing fit, unable to handle the spicy hot food. "Are you O.K.? It's too hot?"

He finally recovered after he coughed loudly. His voice suddenly became high and strained. "Oh, yeah. It -- it...wasn't hot at first."

Annie continued, as she wanted to change the subject since he probably was embarrassed. "I was talking to my friend about how happiness is not created from other people's unhappiness."

Jim, his voice still strained, whispered, "Oh, yeah, that's right."

"Ian agreed it wouldn't be right. Piper would be so unhappy and mad."

At last, Jim seemed to recover his voice, "Oh, so he said it was O.K.?"

"Not quite..." replied Annie. "He said she would kill him."

"Not literally. Just figuratively," said Jim, trying to make it better.

"I don't know," said Annie, not convinced. "I heard about a Buddhist nun killing someone sometime. Maybe it was just a movie." She didn't want to bring this up, but it seemed logical, with all the violence happening in the world. I don't think that would ever happen, she said to herself, so she wouldn't worry about Piper.

I'm not hungry, she said, feeling a bit sick over the conversation...I don't know why, but opposites attract sometimes."

"Oh, do you mean about–Ian?" he said, matter-of-factly.

"I'm sorry, I wanted to stay off the subject."

Jim seemed to be having such a good time it didn't really matter to him. "Did you ever say, 'Go to hell' or 'fuck you' to your mom?" he said, smiling, so matter-of-factly that Annie had no idea what brought up that thought. At that point she was hoping the date would end as soon as possible. Then Jim asked another somewhat strange question, "Is your sister's husband white?"

"Yeah, he is." Not feeling too great, she listened to Jim's response.

"My sister's husband is white. He's into this strange Buddhist chant. Nam myoho renge kyo. He tried to get me to chant. He looks like a Buddhist. And you know, those Presbyterians. They're all the same. You know, those cookie cutter Christians."

"What makes you think they're all that way?" asked Annie, put off about his remark. He stopped and ate his dinner. Annie chanted nam myoho renge kyo whenever she had the spare time. And it helped her be happy.

She jumped back to the present.

"Oh, he's quiet, reserved," said Jim, describing his brother-in-law.

"Is that what makes him look like a Buddhist?" she asked, trying in vain to figure how his brain worked. Wondering how he thought of this, she didn't want to start a conflict.

After a pause, he responded.

"He's just using you."

Just to make sure, she asked, "You mean, Ian?"

He nodded. "Yeah, *that* guy. From what you tell me about him, he's bad-tempered and impatient," he replied. "It's too bad he can't move back to Huntington Beach. And be with his girlfriend." Another strange awkward silence.

Jim poured one cup of soy sauce on top of his food. Annie was taken aback. "Wow---you use a lot of soy sauce." "I love it, yeah. I love teriyaki sauce, peanut sauce...soy sauce..."

He continued on with his put-down about Ian, "He's cheating on his girlfriend...I don't know if that's good or bad. The Zen master I saw at the Buddhist temple told me that if you think tight pants are bad, that's all your outlook on it. It's your perspective."

"That's all he talked to you about?" she asked, trying to believe what she was hearing. "Some deep, profound meaning about tight pants?" That was about the highlight of their evening conversation. She was still trying to make sense of it.

They finally arrived back at her condo. So far so good. At least he's a gentleman about it. It's worth a try, she thought. I guess I'll let him in. But I don't really feel anything, she said to herself as

Jim spoiled her by massaging her feet.

Afterwards, Annie and Jim kept their distance. No sparks or fireworks happening there. Then the unexpected happened. He sat down next to her and put his hand down her back while trying to reach below towards her behind. Repulsed, she stopped abruptly, then pushed his hand away. It caused an unwelcome shiver to go down her spine.

She hated the feeling of his hand wandering on a sensitive area of her body. Later she would feel proud she was able to protect herself, while making up her mind about how she felt with Jim. "I really have something else I have to do tonight." He stood up and got ready to leave.

"Did you take a shower?" Annie suddenly commented. "What's that smell?" she asked, suddenly nauseated.

"Oh, I did, I' m clean."

"But it smells." She wrinkled her nose.

"Oh, I'm wearing cologne. It's expensive cologne."

"That's what it is. I thought it was sweat!"

"No," he said, proudly. Like a show-off. Like it appealed to other people and made him feel sexy. "It's seventy dollars a bottle. It's fruity, like a citrus scent. With some lavender thrown in."

"Lavender? I thought that was a perfume scent for women, mostly…."

With this, he tried to kiss her. She didn't let him. A great come down line, she used it to feel safe.

"I usually never kiss on the first date." She made the perfect excuse. "This isn't the first date," he smiled.

Annie was adamant. "I know," she replied, smirking. After he walked out the door, she locked the door immediately. She felt relieved, like a heavy boulder was lifted off of her shoulders.

So this is what he is like. He doesn't feel like the *one*, thought Annie. Not even close. It was just a reason for her to stay away from Ian.

Chapter Twenty

Josh gets out of his car at Kate's apartment.

```
            JOSH
    So how is your dating
    going? Find anyone you
    like?

            KATE
    To be honest, no. It will
    take some time. Maybe
    something will happen.
```

The next day after the date, Annie and the others from the studio started in on their yearly picnic at Palisades Park. It was going to be fun. Kids began playing, laughing as they dodged frisbies that aimed in their direction. There was a face painting booth lined up with kids and preteens. All having a good time.

Ian was sitting at a picnic table after loading up his plate full of salad and chicken drumsticks. Annie chose a pasta salad in addition to everything else, and sat across from him. After filling themselves up with all the tasty selections, Annie remarked, "Wow, look at that gorgeous sunset!" Glancing at Laura, Dan and the other cast and crew, who were busy eating and talking over how well the post-production was going for "Take Me Away", she stood and walked discreetly towards the beach, glancing at Ian, a look that turned into a mesmerizing smile. She motioned with a nod to Ian, beckoning him to follow her where a sunset in shades of red and yellow glowed as the afternoon waned. They sat on a bench as they enjoyed the view, a pathway surrounded by sturdy palm trees and the last golden rays of the sky.

"So how was your date with Jim?" asked Ian. He couldn't resist hearing the details. She took a deep breath in and sighed. She thought she may as well be honest with him.

"Hmmm," she breathed out. "I don't want to date a guy who wears expensive, smelly perfume on his face," she began, glancing forward and shaking her head.

"I had another date with him just to make sure, and when he was driving me home I said to myself, this is going to end soon. I took a deep breath in and held it all the way, his car smelled so bad. I thought to myself, take me home, take me home, awww, thank goodness, I'm home. I won't be smelling his ugly car again."

Ian chuckled a little as she described it, leaning closer to her. She thought to herself, he's really sexy. And he, as well, thought, she really is funny sometimes. *I wonder why I don't laugh so much about it as much as I should.*

"You see, I don't know if I even *like* him, Ian. I'm not trying to string him along." She paused. She put her palms together and shook them. "I prayed silently, get me out of here, get me out of here, get me out of here, I am almost home, almost home. This is the last date with him, the absolute last date… whew, it was over."

"What did you do after that?" he said, as he glanced at her. She shook her head and stretched back on the bench. "I grabbed the door handle to his car and got myself out of there. And just to be polite, I said a brief thank you and walked quickly back to my condo unit."

"Hah," he chuckled. Yes, definitely funny. He had to admit he enjoyed sitting next to her as he gazed straight ahead towards the glowing sky, that was turning purple next to the golden rays that illuminated the elegant palm trees. Like the time when they filmed the movie.

He felt like leaning closer to her and stealing a kiss, but the others from the office would be watching them. He didn't like gossip at his job. She tried to resist putting her hand over his. Their fingers touched, but that was as far as it got. If Laura or Dan saw them, it might generate some bad feelings in the organization of the company they worked for. Or maybe she was being too paranoid. Still, there was no denying the attraction they felt for each other. They snuck in a hug before anyone could see, after a quick glance at the others.

"I better get back," she said, pulling away. "I need to talk to

Gayle about something. She was having a problem with her husband and I want to see if she's coping better these days. He took hold of her hand and she extended hers, then dropped it quickly as she turned away. More commitment stuff, and she knew it.

"Hey Ian, I'll see you at work." Then bending over towards him, she whispered, "Don't let on we've been with each other."

"Annie, you're the one whose been talking to people."

"I know, I know," she continued to whisper to Ian. She turned suddenly to see Gayle coming towards her. She stood up and her back to Ian, greeted her friend.

"Gayle, how *are* you? How are you and Charles doing?" She said that last part in a whisper.

Gayle laughed. "It's just funny how you whispered that. No, it's fine, we can talk about it." She smiled at Ian. "Charles and I are dating again. He told me he couldn't find anyone else he really cared about more than me and him." She smiled again, warmly.

Annie beamed back at the good news, then gave Gayle a hug. "Oh, I am so happy for you, Gayle! That's great!" Ian extended his hand to Gayle. After Annie introduced them, she gave a slightly jealous look at both of them. They were both, after all, committed to someone. Annie was the only one in the middle.

Noticing Annie, who was feeling awkward standing there between them in the middle, with the two back and forth trading thoughts about how the Penchant/Atlas merger had changed the company, Gayle said "I need to taste a bite of that cherry cheesecake before someone else does." She smiled her goodbye and cheerfully went in the direction off towards the picnic tables.

The next few days Annie had made a decision. She would congratulate herself for being bold. She didn't like the situation she was in with Jim. It was awkward. What seemed funny before was the realization she would have to move on. She wasn't obligated to do what she planned to do, but just so she didn't leave him dragging on, she called Jim.

"Hi Jim? Yeah Jim, I just wanted to say….," as carefully as she could, "I value our friendship, but we're just not compatible."

"What do you mean?! How are we not compatible?"

"I don't want to hurt your feelings…we're just not right for each other."

"But what do you mean we're not compatible?"

"We're just not *compatible*."

"But you haven't told me! Why are we not compatible?" She could hear the anxiousness in his voice and it made her even more annoyed.

"Maybe you don't remember, but you said you didn't know if I was the girl for *you*."

"My mom is just happy that I have a girlfriend!" Annie felt the same way the first time he said this to her. And even now, she didn't think they were exactly girlfriend-boyfriend.

"We're too similar. Both of us hoard stuff. That could be a real problem in the future." As if scared away and panicked, he hung up the phone. Annie sighed, but secretly she felt relief. She did ruminate a little, that if she hadn't said that last part about hoarding, maybe it would have been better, but it sure made it easier to break up quickly. Stop with the thinking like that, you did the right thing, she said to herself, firmly.

The next day, Annie got an email from Jim. It started out like: You always hurt the ones who love you. You are so cold and you lied to me. I thought you were my girlfriend….She hit the delete button, unable to finish reading the email. Later, she wished she had read the whole thing, but it probably would have made her feel lousy, so she was right about not giving it a thorough read.

And he *had* said, "I don't know if you're the girl for me!" during the time they were dating. She did feel she made the right decision. If there was one thing she learned from her experience with Bill, and what he told her when she was dating him, was to not settle for less.

Chapter Twenty-one

> JOSH
> Maybe we better not meet
> like this, Kate. I mean,
> I made a commitment to
> Trudy, and...
>
> KATE
> I just thought we could
> work it out. I mean, at
> least we have a
> friendship. But if
> that's your decision
> I respect that.

Annie went over to her parents' house, just a short walk from where her condominium was, to visit her mother. She was watching television, relaxed on the couch. It was a familiar scene, her mother, who had her back leaning against a fluffed-up pillow. She was glad her mom was able to take it easy at times in her retirement years from working at the hospital as an anesthesiologist. She w3as 85 years old and still an active driver, shopper, cook and cleaner for herself and Mr. Chen, Annie's father. Her relaxation time was well deserved.

When she saw the distress in Annie's eyes, she turned off the TV.

"Mom, Ian's alright. He's a good guy…it's just that…." Tears ran down her face as she talked over what she had never opened up to her mother about Ian. She never opened up about her personal life to her mother, who often blamed the men she herself knew in her life. "He's taken already. I can't see him anymore…."

She thought her mom would look down at her, seemingly putting the man's needs before her own. Her mother tried to teach Annie to be independent, and not care what other people thought of her. Nan Hua didn't like to see Annie showing her weak side.

"Don't cry," she frowned, "it doesn't solve anything," not moving from her spot.

"I know, I can't….Ian is getting married….and I can't do anything about it…" She paused, then asked herself, why are you crying? Why are you so weak? Stop crying, you're upsetting your mom! she heard a voice inside say.

"Oh, come on, Annie…," she heard her mother say, in the way Annie knew she would react. "You're stronger than that! Why do you have to cry! Over a *man*!" She said that last part indignantly. Annie immediately felt sheepish, and dried her tears. Yup. She knew that was going to come from her mother, even before it happened.

"OK, I need to let them be. Let them be happy," said Annie, pulling herself together. "Happiness does not come from others' unhappiness," she repeated, remembering one of her friend's words of advice.

She reached out to hug her mother, who smiled gently and stood up, saying, "Come on. Stop crying. Look, I want to show you something," as she walked to her bedroom.

Her mother took out a package of clothing in a clear plastic bag that she was "hiding" under her bed. Annie was always happy when her mom bought clothes for her, even if they weren't her style. She had bags of Care package clothing her mother had given her that were mostly too big or a not so flattering color on her. It was the thought of her gesture that moved her, so she didn't care what her mother had bought, it was all coming from the heart.

"You don't worry. Don't care what he does. You have your own life. Your body is your own!" as she unzipped a jacket in an odd shade of blue for her, and motioned for her daughter to put her arms in the jacket. She smiled even when she saw it was two sizes too big for her. She would bundle up in layers of sweaters and wear the coat inside. She had fond memories of department stores she would get lost in because her mom loved shopping so much she would disappear in the store, much to Annie's chagrin. She couldn't count the number of times she had to ask the store clerk for help finding her.

"Mrs. Chen, could you please meet your daughter, Annie at the front desk?" she asked the store associate to announce.

Her mom was busy looking at stuff she didn't need, and getting lost in the ladies changing rooms, not finding anything she liked. She had to look through the entire store for her mom, aisle by aisle and clothing rack by clothing rack, because she wasn't responding to the store clerk's PA system announcement. Mother and daughter would beam at each other when she would finally show up at the front of the store, after her little shopping adventure.

Despite the little inconveniences, it was sometimes warm and fun shopping with her mom. She would allow Annie to choose one article of clothing per trip in their shopping adventure.

And her dad. Annie was deeply respectful towards her father, a university professor at the local university. As a child, there wasn't much time for him to be with his daughters, with the demands of traveling for lectures, writing recommendations for his former students, even hosting a party for expert readers and consultants on a famous Chinese novel. So now in his retirement years, he embraced that change.

M.W., her father's nickname of his Chinese name Ming Wen, meaning Bright Scholar, had read a few scenes from one of her writing projects, and called it "propaganda". Although her father may not have understood the subject matter in her screenplays, or why she wanted to write a certain way, she remembered the times when she helped him to translate his poems from Mandarin to English. She cherished those moments.

She knew her parents didn't have a picture-perfect

relationship. Or so it was while they were all living together. Annie blamed herself sometimes for being a burden on them.

"Your dad only cares about his career. He didn't take time to spend with his family while he was working, even in between the speeches he made at those universities, like at Hong Kong University." Annie could feel the resentment in her voice. I think she was longing for some gesture of love between them.

Annie brooded. "I'm sure he cares about you, Mom," was the best she could say, looking down at her shoes. She wasn't a marriage counselor. Lift your head up when you say that, Annie Chen, she reminded herself. You just need more confidence in yourself.

"If he really cared he wouldn't be off in his own little world carving Chinese seals and reading books."

"But Mom, he just enjoys doing those things. He's a professor. He's not purposely trying to ignore you," Annie tried to explain.

"Always on *his* side, I know," she would remark, bitterly. Even when Annie insisted she wasn't taking sides.

She reminded her mother that just earlier this year, her dad had bought a velvet heart cushion for her mother with the words, "I love you" in Chinese characters for Valentine's Day. She even dug around in her mom's closet to find it, and showed it once again to Nan Hua. Even Annie was surprised at this sweet show of affection.

"You see, Mom, Dad really loves you," said Annie, reassuring her mom. Her mom was silent, but she had a peaceful, content look on her face.

And for herself, M.W. had said, "Annie, you can talk to me about anything that is bothering you. I heard from your mom about that man, Bill. You be careful. I am always here to stand up for you, Annie."

It was that way with Ian's dad, Walter, too. He was protective of his son even more after meeting Piper for the first time. It was a cold autumn day in November, when Ian brought Piper to his parents' house to introduce her to them. "Ian, can you tell them to turn up the heat? It's really cold in here!" spoiled Piper insisted, without bothering to acknowledge them, say hello, or even greet his parents right in front of them.

His stepmother was an Okinawan, Sashiko, who Walter had met years ago on a business trip to Japan. She was sincerely trying to be polite to her guest, but Piper was treating her like a servant, in her own home.

Sashiko went into the kitchen to offer her some cookies and tea. Piper stopped her, "No, no cookies for me. I am trying to keep a flat stomach. Ian, can you please tell her I can't have any of that sugar? Tell her for me, she might not understand my English." What an embarrassment for Ian and his family.

After Piper had gone home, Walter told Ian his opinion of Piper. "She's pushy and demanding. Your mom was just trying to be nice to her. You know, after her looks fade away, what will she have left? I don't see anything in her. You can do better than that, Ian."

Instead of agreeing, Ian defended her. "She's just a little high-strung at times. She just thought Mom didn't know much English. Maybe she had mom or daddy issues, I don't know."

But he never wanted to bring that up with Piper, knowing full well she would just have a temper tantrum. Ian tried to take his father's criticisms with a grain of salt. It's only natural that a dad would be protective of his son, he reassured himself. He was going to get married. To Piper. It was. high time for that and he wasn't going to let his dad get in the way of his decision.

Chapter Twenty-two

    KATE (to her mother, Julia)
I stopped dating that guy,
Josh. He's made a
commitment to her. It's
time for me to start over.

        JULIA
Now you're talking like a
sensible person. You don't
need to cry over anyone.

        KATE
But then again, I haven't
found anyone else.
        (she pauses)
    Yet.

        JULIA
Kate, I just want you to
be happy! OK?

        KATE
OK, Mom.

Kate gives her mother a kiss.

Annie went for her morning walk, increasing to a fast jog, her heart beating in glowing health, and felt determined. She was making a fresh start, or so she thought. At home, she moved over to her computer, turned it on, and quickly erased all of Ian's e-mails to her. The one about how he would love to come over because he couldn't stop thinking about her. And the one he wrote in joyful response to a digital greeting card of a panda she sent and how he felt the same attraction she was feeling. She made sure the large box of underwear was going back. And I feel so silly in those frilly bras and panties. She made a note to herself.

She was going to take care of this hoarding thing. Opening her closets, about sixty-six pieces of clothing she collected over the span of three years fell out and onto the floor. She hastily filled fifteen grocery bags of these and the twelve pairs of high heels that hurt her feet.

The following week she had the Salvation Army guys come by to pick up all the unnecessary clothing. As she piled up the bags for them to take out, paper bags tore and fell over onto the carpeted condo hallway.

"Ma'am, we can come back another time," one of them said. Annie ignored the comment and she kept finding more to give away, high heeled pumps that caused her back pain and bunion pain, combat boots from her punk days, stuff made out of fabric so old her mom bought for her that they were worn out, faded and stiff.

"Whoa!" the other guy said, bewildered but amused. He whistled loudly when she kept putting bags out into the hallway for them, the almost desperate last-minute decisions based on her goal of keeping her entire closet minimal.

And as for her relations with her sister, Annie didn't want Kay to worry about her. They rarely got together except for the ubiquitous family gatherings like Chinese New Year's and Christmas. Annie was hoping her visits with Kay would deepen the understanding between them. Sometimes it just seemed like they were perpetually at odds with each other.

On the one hand, Kay was pragmatic and sensible, always trying to enlighten Annie to more common sense, and on the other hand, Annie, the dreamer, thought that things may magically change or improve in a relationship. Nothing wrong with that, but she got herself in a rut often in her clashes with others, being born in the sign of the stubborn, hardworking Ox, supposedly. Kay, born in the year of the Dog, was steadfastly loyal to her family.

Now they sat at a restaurant in Santa Monica. Kay insisted on being the big sis, treating Annie to lunch. Annie was going to take this opportunity to open up about her decision regarding Ian.

"I think it's best that Ian doesn't move in with me. Thanks for the advice, Kay. Otherwise, it would be like him having two girlfriends."

"How can he have two girlfriends?" said Kay. The thought of it was still mind-boggling to her.

"It's really not like he has two girlfriends. It seems I made a mistake of getting involved with him, but it really wasn't my fault. When I asked who was taking care of his cat, he simply said, "I have a girl…taking care of my cat." I thought he had a professional catsitter who was a girl!" Annie felt a little foolish recalling this.

She knew Kay would offer her advice to get him out of her place, so Annie said, quickly, to change the subject, "This is good food!" She gobbled down her clam chowder, trying to get over the fact she didn't want to be told what to do. She anticipated what was coming.   "You need to take care of yourself. If that relationship isn't working for you, it's best you don't keep it going," she said, solemnly.

"Hey thanks for this lunch. It isn't often I get invites to eat out, with work and all." She wanted to change the subject, desperately. She knew her sister better than that. It was no use trying to change Kay's mind, at least not at the moment.

"Please don't feel guilty about your decision," said Kay, her strict advice changing to warm concern for her younger sister.

"Oh no, no guilt at all. I feel free now," Annie said, her easygoing manner getting the better of her stubborn side. "Annie, I say those things for your own happiness."

"Yes, I know. Don't worry. I'm working on it. Me and Ian are still friends now, though. I'm OK with it." She downed her sparkling water and watched for Kay's reaction. Kay probably hoped I wouldn't ever want to see Ian again, she turned over in her mind. That would be impossible anyway, because Ian was working for the same company she worked for. And that was fine with Annie. She wanted to stay friends with him.

When she returned home, she made a cup of coffee for herself and relaxed in front of the tube. She put on an old '80's movie and had a laugh at the comedy, a romantic comedy that followed the escapades of a woman's dating adventures brought to light trying to find her true love. And right then and there the phone rang. It was Ian.

"I've got to put on my makeup, then we can go out," she said, as if it was natural that they should connect with each other. He was quickly becoming her best friend.

"How are you Annie?" He paused and asked slyly, "What are you wearing? I should just come over." Something about his bad boy attitude attracted her. Or was it sweet rebellion after many years of being treated unfairly, as if you were never enough. Never shapely enough, strong enough, trim enough, capable enough as the next woman. Always the other woman, when Plan A didn't work out. This time she wanted to be number one to somebody. Whether or not it worked out with Ian.

"Annie, you're allergic to that makeup," he retorted. "Take that junk off your face. You don't need that stuff." They both paused, as if deciding whether or not this was a good idea.

"I moved into another place. My neighbor is a Chinese guy. He's cool."

There was no stopping them. Every other date was nothing to her. No passion or understanding was fulfilled by other guys she knew, or whom she had met. She realized she had been trying to forget about Ian. But she was in too deep. Annie said, abruptly, "I wanna come over. Now." She put on her coat and left her place. It didn't matter how late it was at night, or how dark it was. She wanted to be with Ian.

Walking on the dark pavement, she lit her way with a small flashlight that came with a discount bag she bought. She knocked on the door of where he lived. It was amazing that she knew where she was going, she was so bad with street names and directions. The door on the side of the house he lived in led to a small converted room.

He lived in basically the basement of a house the owner rented out to two people, Ian and the Chinese student, Hu Zhi who rented the other converted room.

His neighbor was on his computer when she arrived. She felt his eyes on her, wondering and imagining what was going to happen next. Ian opened the door a crack, stopped and stared at Annie before she walked in. He closed the door, then went back to playing a video game on his laptop. He turned to her, gave her a hug, then took out a DVD and showed it to her.

"This is such a cheesy movie. You know, Rae Dawn Chong is in it. You're Rae Dawn Chong." She smirked and shook her head, amused at his naive fantasy. "No, I'm not. I'm not anything like her." He went back to his laptop computer and looked at it.

"I'm sorry Annie, I'm just listening to music. I'm into this, Annie." He let the heavy metal blast from the speakers. "I went to rock concerts in high school. Hair down to here."

He pointed past his shoulders. "I was into this starting from high school."

"I know all about that," she said. "I used to sing and play electric guitar in a rock band during college in Michigan." He came up to her and started to kiss her neck as she sat on his bed.

"I don't care what anyone else thinks. There's nothing wrong here," she said, with a rebellious smile. "Why should you care? It's none of their goddamn business what we do." She hugged him, with her arms around him, moving upwards to massage the back of his neck. "I don't feel guilty …. you're not married!"

Ian replied, "We're not even having sex!"

They kissed and hugged, as if this was a way to feel better about the situation. "Just think," said Ian, "if you had this every night." Then, as if rethinking the situation, he pulled away from Annie. "Let's go to my place, now," she said. He hastily put on his jacket and they walked, arm in arm, Annie lighting the way with her tiny flashlight.

"I think we're both lonely," said Ian, as they took the short and familiar path back to her place. "I hope I don't see my neighbors, Mr. and Mrs. Li. I mean, they're nice people but they gossip a lot," said Annie, cautiously. "Mr. Li always frowns when he sees me bringing friends over and acts irrational sometimes. He pounds the wall if I have the TV on too loud."

Fortunately no one was in sight. It was late, after all. Finally in the warm comfort of her home, they watched a movie, side by side again on the floor. He tried to kiss her more, but she drew away and went to sleep on her bed. She wasn't going to risk getting her emotions trampled on. He was going to be with Piper any day now. She was smarter than that.

"I'm just a horny boy," he said, as he turned to his other side and slept right there on the carpet. Annie thought, gazing at him, he looks cute on his side, sleeping on the floor. No, she wasn't going to risk it. Soon he was going to be engaged. She didn't want to know the details.

Chapter Twenty-three

                    KATE
          I'm too busy to worry
          about my love life,
          Kimiko.

Kate's friend, Kimiko nods her
head.

                    KIMIKO
          Don't worry about it.
          It's got to come
          naturally. Just let it
          happen.

                    KATE
          I think I need to keep
          looking. Instead of
          worrying.

"In this scene she has the scarf on wrong. In the last scene it was

draped differently. And that cup has moved. We need the same

cups and plates we had in our last shot," Gayle said to the

production assistants. She was working in Continuity in addition to being Script Supervisor. "Annie, you remember, don't you? And also she was sitting here, not standing," she motioned towards the leading actress.

Annie quickly moved the dishes into the previous positions, then directed the starring actress to the place she was sitting before.

"Let's take a break right now," said Charles, after they completed two more takes. Charles was happily signed on again to take the coveted job as director in this new production, "Kate's Kisses", produced by Nine Figure Pictures. "We need to recharge the equipment and recharge ourselves for the rest of the afternoon," he said as he headed towards lunch at the catering tables.

Annie took the initiative to talk to Gayle. "You know I still have feelings for Ian. I mean, according to the Chinese zodiac, we're the perfect match for each other ..." Half expecting a put-down at this rather superstitious or naïve remark, she was surprised that Gayle didn't laugh at her or become sarcastic.

Smiling, she told Annie, "You have to put yourself first from now on and love you, because you, Annie, are a diamond." Happy that her friend was showing some compassion, she listened as Gayle opened up about her dating life. "I've met some guys, and--they're nice guys, but...." Gayle knew Annie's heart, so she said, "I know you're lonely. There are a lot of nice guys. But with my husband, Charles, I knew it was right. Finding the one for you has to come naturally."

After shooting finished for the day, Annie decided to take a drive to Topanga State Park, 13 minutes away from her home. Sun came in between oak tree branches in one of her favorite places in the world. Their swaying leaves left shimmering light on the path's walkway. She was impelled to call Ian.

"Hey, Ian, how are you?"

He paused. "I'm taking business law classes. I love it."

"I hope all your dreams come true and you reach all your goals," she said.

"You're the one that has to make *your* dreams come true!" he said, with empathy. "I'll always be your little Rooster," he added, gently.

"I'll always be your little Ox," said Annie.

"Where were you when I needed you," His voice trailed. "… when I was searching for the right one. If only we knew each other before all this." He changed his tune, then. She liked how he was romantic and practical at the same time.

"Maybe we can go shopping. I can't read the Chinese on the packages." Then, with a moment's thought, not hesitating, he said, "I think you should not have sex at all with a guy, not until after marriage."

"What? In this day and age? Is it possible?" she answered, slightly sarcastic.

"Just wait until after the marriage."

"O.K...Thanks," she responded, knowing full well he didn't

even have that kind of relationship with Piper. But despite this, she was rather impressed that her and Ian never had sex with each other apart from hugs and kisses. At least he's showing he cares and respects me.

She suddenly remembered something. "Hey, there's a cougar convention happening at the Oceanside Hotel. I heard about it over the radio." She expected him to be amused, which he was, breaking into a smile.

"Yeah, you do seem to like younger guys," he teased, wondering why he didn't realize it at first. "A cougar convention?" He slowly began to picture it. "You should go! Maybe we should go together," he said, thoughtfully.

"Ahem," she growled, "the point is in me going *alone*. To meet guys."

"You mean to meet cubs. You're the cougar. I wanna go with you. I'll be your bodyguard," he said, only half-jokingly. "I've got nothing better to do on the weekend."

Chapter Twenty-four

                KATE
    Sometimes dating is fun.
    When you're still single.
    It makes you feel like
    you're in your twenties
    again.

                KIMIKO
    Oh, yeah?
            (she laughs)
    Pick and choose as you
    please, you mean?

                KATE
    Or just have fun flirting?
    I'm not married, anyway.

                KIMIKO
    Go for it!

Pounding, hypnotic dance pop music played as Annie entered the prestigious hotel, Ian walking behind her through the conference doors. She was looking for adventure, and he was feeling dragged along, but on the lookout for trouble if Annie ever got into any.

Cougar women, in their 40's and up were pounding the carpet in their ultra-high sexy heels, wine glasses in hands. Cubs were in their twenties up to mid-thirties, already sitting between women, two or three at a time, being spoilt by cougar ladies offering them fruit plates and Reisling white wine from the catered tables outside of the conference rooms.

The rented rooms were converted into a club-like setting. The ladies at the event had an average dress length of 28" from shoulder down to crotch line.

"These cougar women are really having a good time!" shouted Annie to Ian, who was sitting hunched with a can of beer. Annie herself was dressed in a close-hugging pink minidress that complimented her dark framed eyeglasses.

Unlike Annie, Ian was wondering when the foolishness would end. But cubs were evidently having a good time, too, their youthful arms wrapped around the shapely ladies who tried to resemble young adult women. Or some of them reveled in their shapely, more mature bodies, with more muscular, full-figured thighs.

"Oh wait! There's Jackie!" sounded off Annie, pointing to one of the main conference rooms. "I read about her online, she really knows her cougar stuff!"

"Shhhh! You don't have to shout, I can hear you." Despite his efforts, Ian gave up trying to get Annie to pipe down and relax. He just rolled his eyes instead. "Where's the food?" he winced. "In here!!" shouted Annie over the music, pointing to the reception area in the back of the conference room. There was enough fresh finger food, beer and wine to keep him happy for the rest of the afternoon.

A trim and tall blonde lady in a lowcut, form-fitting light blue business jacket and miniature pencil skirt addressed the crowd. Her white studded pumps complemented her shapely legs, as she strode back and forth on a stage. Ian made his way quietly over to the snack part of the lunch table.

"You made it to our annual Cougar Cub Get-Together!" she started the introduction. "I'm Jackie, I'll be your host for today." Cheers and whistles came from the audience.

"We're proving that there's nothing wrong with us cougar ladies loving younger men who don't die on us, don't use Viagra, or end up in a wheelchair!"

The partygoers cheered in wild applause. "Congratulations to all of you for making it here today! You cougar ladies are lookin' good! I'm sure you all are buzzing about our packed schedule full of cougar and cub dating advice, how a cub learns to take care of his aging old lady in heels, how cougar women learn to protect their cubs from being stolen by younger women. Are there any couples out there who would like to speak about their experiences? What struck you, what attracted you to each other?"

Annie nudged Ian. But Ian looked annoyed and shook his head. "Noooo, I don't wanna say anything…." he mumbled to Annie.

A cougar woman in her fifties stood up with her young man.

"You won't believe how I met this guy," she said, head turned at a provocative angle. She stood up straight, showing off her busty profile. "He was a student in an extension program cooking class I took. I'll just say I stayed longer in the ladies room than I thought I would, during break…," to which the crowd whistled, then some moaned and even booed. A mixed reaction. Some of them, Annie included, laughed and felt a little embarrassed.

An attractive older woman stood up, smiled, and urged her younger man, to stand up, also. "I'm Marilyn, and this is…" Her date remained seated, but finally stood up as she gave his name. "Mike."

"We've been together, up to the present moment, for nine years!" she boasted. The party people cheered. "We just love to shock people. You know, some people think he's my son. They're a little surprised when they find out we're having sex!"

The crowd whistled at this rather crude commentary, eager to hear more. "It's true. We're having a great time, and we're even thinking of having threesomes…"

Immediately, Mike cut her off. "This is the reason why I thought we better cool it with our relationship …"

"But honey, this morning you…"

He announced, "O.K. We need some face time about this. All those weird people you met on the internet? They all heard about our private sex life. I had to tell them you were an ex-prostitute and that was the reason you wanted sex with them. Just to drive them away. Then the opposite happened. They started flirting with you." The look on her face was appalling.

"You! You..!! How could you!!" The party animals' reactions were mixed. "Break up with her, come to my house!" and from the moderator, "Jackie, can you get control of this, now?"

Caught off-guard, Jackie fielded these comments. "OK, folks...let's move on to my second point...how to stay together..." Ian whispered to Annie, "This is dumb. Let's get out of here, now."

"No, it's getting interesting." Annie couldn't wait to see what happened next. Marilyn shouted at the poor guy, "You little tramp! Bad cub, bad!" while poor defenseless Mike raised his hands to fend off her face slaps.

As Annie's jaw dropped, out of the corner of her eye she watched as a few couples were talking to each other about this outbreak. Some others were numb in shock. He looks familiar, thought Annie, eyeing a tall man listening to the couple's arguments. Looks like Jim. No, it couldn't be. Wait. "It *is* Jim," she said, under her breath, with Magnolia by his side.

Annie, wishing to stay anonymous, stared at his limping leg and noticed he had an accident with his foot with a cast on. Apparently not in pain. Ian noticed her gawking at Jim, stopped and asked, "What's going on?" She lowered her voice to a whisper in Ian's ear.

"It's Jim...you know, the would-be writer. You remember. Nice guy Jim. I think he broke his foot dancing," when she decided to be friendly and say hello. Magnolia narrowed her eyes and gave her a look that she didn't like Annie butting in.

Magnolia, well-endowed and wearing a European-designed dress, did happen to look well that early evening and she gave Annie back another look that was just as sharp. According to Jim, she lived just ten months in the US and only married Peter for a green card.

"She divorced Peter just a week ago. We're celebrating her freedom!" said Jim, cheerfully. Ian came up, with a bottle of Rolling Rock, side by side with Annie.

Just to be polite, she said, "And this is my friend, Jim, and Magnolia. Magnolia sells designer jeans." Wishing to get out of there as soon as possible after another particularly long, sharp look from Magnolia, Annie followed Ian towards the main double doors.

Then to Annie's dismay, she watched Jim get up to join the others in a room where another workshop instructor was giving her talk. But he was alone. I guess he likes cougar women, I wonder what happened to Magnolia?

A few older ladies came over to sit next to him, and it looked like they were engaging in some friendly conversation. "Whaddyou do to your foot, young man? An accident?" one of the ladies in platform heels asked. She really did look about twenty years younger, except for a few extra wrinkles, although she may have had plastic surgery for that. Annie overheard her volunteering to buy him a drink. I'm glad Jim seems to be enjoying himself. He's a nice enough guy, I'm just not attracted to him though ....

"Oh hi Annie!" He suddenly broke his silence and turned his attention to Annie. She just as quickly changed her mind about Jim. Should have stopped staring at him. Now I know why Ian wanted to get out of there. Release me from this place.

"Hey, Annie, I found out you were going to this party." It wasn't a party, she thought, emphatically, almost wanting to correct him.

And she almost wanted to ask what he was doing there but it flashed in her mind, of course, to meet cougars, like me, as Jim made his way over to her. How did he manage to find out I was going to be here? Something strange here. It wasn't like she told friends she was interested in any upcoming event. She would have remembered that. But she did still list him as a friend on facebook. Just as she was making a reminder to herself to unfriend him online, she saw busty lady Magnolia having a drink by herself.

"Is Jim ignoring you, Magnolia? I saw him just now with all those babes around him." Magnolia stared at Annie, not saying a word. "It's OK, Magnolia. I've got a date, a friend I'm with. I'm not after Jim if that's what you think."

Then she surprised herself by saying to Magnolia, "I'm sure if you ask you could even go away with him, take yourself away from here on vacation." Magnolia's eyes were darting from Annie to Jim, as if trying to see if there was actually any truth to that.

Before Magnolia could think of launching a belittling and berating lecture back at Annie, she said, "Magnolia, *you're* so much more the better match for Jim than me. I just had a friendship with him. Stick with him, you won't regret it." Magnolia kept staring, then had another hefty sip of her drink, and finally downed the rest in a few seconds. "And, Magnolia, let him know you're not letting him go. Let him know you're serious about him. Ask him to take you away somewhere. Anywhere romantic. He'll do it, I know Jim."

She watched as her eyes grazed the dance floor and landed on Jim, and Magnolia promptly butt in when Jim and an older lady dressed like a high school student in a plaid skirt and cropped top, extended her hand for Jim to join her in a dance. Jim refused, he and Magnolia soon nestled closely with each other, and it looked like she was following Annie's advice, to her relief. But no, I'm not a matchmaker, she said, firmly to herself. They weren't off on their own. Not just yet. Just outside the doors, a familiar-looking man took a hit from his roach, leaning against the walls.

Peter, looking a little bored, but just as happy being on his own, was getting stoned. Wonder why he isn't with a woman, Annie mulled over in her mind. Maybe another lover who was into what he thought were the joys of toking. It wasn't impossible. Here again, Annie quickly reminded herself she wasn't put on the planet to be a matchmaker. She couldn't help noticing, though. The woman with the plaid skirt, and tottering around on her heels, gave up on Jim and gave an eye scan to Ian, purring, "Hey there, hon, do you want a drink?"

Ian drew his head out of view and said to Annie, quickly,

"Let's leave!" This time Ian said it out loud. He headed for the door. The lady started to move in on Peter, who was patiently waiting, still getting stoned. "May I trouble you to have a hit of that, honey? I haven't had one since 1979." To which Peter reached out to help the lady inhale. Annie almost practically fled the scene, leaving them to develop their friendship.

"Hold on, Ian," her voice trailed behind him. He started walking outside the doors. She was off by herself for a moment. That is, until she noticed a tall man with chiseled features wearing a cowboy hat, holding his drink. He happened to be hanging out near Annie, and turned to look at her.

"Every time I come here, they get the schedules mixed up. I thought by now they would get that problem fixed."

Attracted to his southern drawl and the way he looked, muscular in his blue chambray button up shirt, which was buttoned down just above where she imagined his six-pack abs might be, she gazed at him from a corner of her eye.

"This is my first time." Annie lowered her voice and peered into his deep blue eyes. "It seems pretty well put together."

"You must be in luck. I've been here five times and still haven't met anyone worth their weight in gold. So far, that is." "I never thought I'd make it here," she said, with honesty. "The speakers are good. I'm drawn to Jackie's spontaneity and sincerity."

"About the only thing good here. My name's John. Yours?"

"Annie," she said, as she extended her hand, admiring the shade of his brown hair, his mustache and goatee. "Nice to meet you." They shook hands. "You came here all by your lonesome?"

"No, I came with my friend." "So what brought you here today?" Annie asked, curiously, at this man in Wrangler jeans. No designer wear on him, at all. Just the down-to-earth, rugged type."Just wanted to see what it was like, compared to last year. I take it all with a grain of salt. I'm amused by the whole cougar thing."

Annie added, "I just came for the experience. I thought it would be fun. And it was." Annie was enjoying his down-home country accent and upbeat manner. Before she knew it, John scribbled his number onto a paper napkin.

"Well, here's my number. Just in case that doesn't work out for ya." He glanced over at Ian with a sideways tilt of his head as Ian walked back to meet Annie.

"Oh we're just friends," she motioned with a look towards Ian. "Here's my number, too. I may take you up on this," she said, handing him her card.

He winked at her and smiled. "I'll see ya."

Ian came up to Annie. "O.K. Let's go." Annie put the napkin in her bag. Ian tried not to let Annie know he heard their conversation. "We've been here all day! I wanna watch one of my movies," he said, impatiently.

"Not one of your samurai movies…," she retorted. She was relieved, because she couldn't wait to take off those heels that were pinching her toes like a masochist. And she told herself, she was not one.

They started to leave, when she turned slightly to look back at John. John watched them go, then smiled and raised his cup to her.

Chapter Twenty-five

At her home office space, after soaking and rubbing her toes, Annie continued on with her screenplay. Sweet release.

                    KATE
          We need to break up. Why
          can't you just leave it
          at that? Don't you believe
          me?

                    JOSH
          Sure I do.

                    KATE
          What did you mean when you
          said we could be together
          in the next lifetime? What
          about this one?

                    JOSH
          No I meant, we knew each
          other in a past lifetime.

Let's go out!

KATE
I have to think about
my career. You're the
one who told me that.

Annie thought to herself while looking over her notes. OK, Josh is still reacting to Kate in a roundabout way. She hoped he would listen when he found out she had a recent marriage proposal. But what she initially was feeling was she wanted to be left alone, however, her heart said she couldn't give up Josh. He was completely blinded over this fact. But the character of Kate was acting with her gut instinct, still. She needed to listen to her heart.

Annie, however, did listen to her heart. And to Ian's advice. When she finally wrote her screenplay into a state of mind she was happy with, she got the courage to attend the Southern California Pitchfest the following summer.

It was a full turnout, with participants bubbling over their screenplay pitch experiences to one another, and plenty of advice covering questions at the packed seminars of this 50-year old annual pitchfest. The writer wannabes formed two straight lines, all of them excited and expectant of their chance to sell their screenplays to major players at the top motion picture studios. They held out more than a glimmer of hope that somehow their feature film scripts would be accepted, with deals made, and careers launched overnight.

Despite the excitement, Annie still felt overwhelmed. She asked some of the other women writers waiting in line if they were nervous, and was surprised to hear many of them were feeling shaky themselves, some even feeling sick about it, too. She didn't know from looking at them. Besides the goal of selling their screenplays, there was the other possibility of getting signed on with an agent. She was beginning to realize that success required you to bring out courage in representing your script, or being noticed as writing talent.

When it was her turn, she approached one of the pitch tables, as an agent finished talking to another aspiring screenwriter. She took one look at Annie and said, "I'm not ready yet," as she shuffled some notes. "OK, you can start," she said, a bit detached. She winced when Annie pitched her idea, to try and make sense of it.

"You're going to have to change it," she said, as Annie defended her work, "But I think my screenplay is good the way it is," while the agent scribbled down the title of a screenwriting book. Here, get this book and read it." A snarky professional, she handed it to Annie, who sneaked away hoping no one noticed.

There was a comfortable couch she sat in, and immediately called Kay to ask if she could send a fax of her logline and synopsis she had forgotten to bring with her. Don't disregard that fact, of Kay being willing to help her, she said to herself. She just had to look at the bright side of their relationship as sisters.

She stood at the concierge counter, while the staff member

received the fax from Kay. Nervously, she thanked the staff member and made off to the pitch tables again, after a quick read-through of the logline, memorizing her sales pitch. This is the time you have to be an extrovert, she remembered from bootcamp.

Annie dragged herself from producer to producer. She grabbed bottles of water as sweat dripped down her forehead. At producer #5(the number she pitched to, or seemingly pitched to, she lost count), she met an older woman face to face. She was close to retirement age. "OK, give it a go," she started, weary from the number of lame pitches she had heard that day. "Girl meets boy, with girlfriend...sometimes love happens in the most unexpected ways." "Where's your synopsis?" Nervous, Annie handed it to her.

Kay was perfect. If she hadn't sent over the fax of her synopsis, it would have been an awkward moment and maybe loss of a sale. "We'll call if we're interested."

Annie pitched again. "Girl meets boy, but already has a girlfriend. Will they find the love they have been waiting for, or is this failed relationship number 100?" Mr. Bing held out his hand for the synopsis. Annie handed it to him. He read it, then announced after a pause, as Annie held her breath .... "We have enough romantic comedies." Annie crossed out "Prodco #8" while cursing him under her breath.

Still another pitch: Prodco #9. "...with a girlfriend ... sometimes love changes ..." Annie started getting a coughing fit. "Water! Water! Water! Water!"

A producer pointed to some water bottles. Annie grabbed one

and chugged it down. She took several and put them into her bag. Annie handed another producer her synopsis.

Annie jotted down: Producer #10... "I don't know if your writing has what it takes, hon." Annie crossed out "Prodco #10".

When you least expect it ..." Annie tore up a sheet with "Prodco #11" on it, gritting her teeth inside. Annie was panting, the sweat dripping over her face, her glasses beginning to slide down her nose.

It's Producer #12. Annie just couldn't stand the smell of her cheap perfume. She mustered up her passion for one more, just one more....

"It's a romantic dramedy.... A woman discovers the man she is attracted to has a girlfriend and has to decide if it's worth it to continue the relationship." The producer glanced through a few of the first three pages, then tossed the rest across the table. Her actions caused Annie's synopsis and logline that she labored over for hours, onto the carpet.

"Oh I am *so* sorry. I'll help you with that," she feigned sweetness. Another producer cut in, "Oh Marsha, your review of that last wonderful screenplay. You outdid yourself, you are a genius in what works and what doesn't..." she was sucking up so hard that the producer immediately sat up and chatted awhile with her. All during this time Annie picked up her papers, cursing under her breath.

"Cross out producer #12, Annie, and don't look back!" She grit her teeth. "I don't know why I put myself through this," Annie thought. "OK, just this once…." She brightened her face, pulled up the corners of her mouth and perked herself up to see producer #13, she lost track of the numbers for a moment.

A petite and charming middle-aged lady asked her, "Do you have a copy of your treatment? I'll take a look at it."

"I have a synopsis, I hope that's OK," Annie said swiftly, on her toes while she handed her a copy. She read the first page and beyond to the second page.

"You know, I really like the concept here. It's unlike anything I've read, at least not today, or the past week. It's kind of funny, too, which is what we're looking for. I'll be in touch," she smiled and shook hands with Annie. Annie, trying to stay calm, blurted, heart pounding, "Nice to meet you."

Boy was that lame, thought Annie. That was all that you could say? Her inner demons needed to be reined in. But this one was the only producer who was genuinely interested.

At work again the next week, during a free moment, Annie jotted a few ideas on index cards for another screenplay. She gave herself a boost of self-confidence. I can do this. I can do this. I can do this. She wasn't going to waste any time while writing her babies. As she finished a one-liner that she scribbled onto a card, a familiar petite lady approached Annie's cubicle.

She extended her hand and said, "Hello, Annie? I'm Barbara, the executive producer. We met at the pitchfest." Annie recognized the woman she had last spoken with. "As we both know, Penchant Pictures just finished the editing for 'Take Me

Away.' Laura, whom I've known for many years on different projects told me you wrote this romantic comedy."

Annie, overjoyed with this opportunity, shook her hand firmly. What should I say? What should I ask? Should I talk about my script? Will I sound like I'm bragging about it? She hated that part of her sometimes.

"I remembered speaking with you about your screenplay. Laura also told me you were really serious about your writing. With your permission, I'd like to option it to some producers I know who may be interested. I like the fact that these people who have so many self-doubts and insecurities in their relationships are marginalized but are given a chance to redeem themselves. Can I ask who gave you the inspiration for this script?"

Without hesitation, she replied, "I have manic depression and obsessive-compulsive disorder. I just wanted to create a character that me and others could relate to." The words fell off her tongue naturally. But after realizing how she opened up about it, she immediately froze inside. There wasn't any turning back now. She continued on.

"But because some people reject some of her behaviors, like reading over lists over and over again, avoiding cracks in the sidewalks, counting things, she can still be in a loving relationship and be happy." She paused, hoping it wouldn't turn her off.

Barbara nodded, "Yes, I can see it is something close to you, about your own experiences, too. I congratulate you on having the courage to do this. I'll be in touch," she smiled, "I'll let you know when I get the greenlight to produce this next feature. I feel confident in this project."

Immediately after she left, Annie jumped for joy in silence and did a virtual happy dance. Finally, after three years of writing and pitching, she broke through. "Annie, could you come by my office?" the familiar voice of Laura came across to her on speakerphone.

Uh oh, hope I didn't do anything wrong. Part of her hated these one-on-one conversations, but she was curious to find out more.

When Annie appeared a minute later, Laura began again, "Yes, I heard that Barbara came by to speak to you about your screenplay. And I wanted to let you know Dan and I have decided to promote you to a story editor position for Nine Figure Pictures. You've been with the company for three years now."

Annie, trying not to hesitate, said, "I know, Laura, I know. But I've been thinking it over. I really enjoy writing my screenplays, and I'm waiting to hear back from Barbara about this script I wrote that means a lot to me…."

Laura nodded, and said, "Yes, Annie. I completely support you on that. You've been working a long time on that piece of work. Have you considered being a full time writer?" She took the opportunity to confirm what was on her mind, and on Laura's, too.

"It's been a dream of mine even before this position opened up for me here."

"Let's see if Barbara can come up with something. Then we'll take it from there. Alright with you?" asked Laura, folding her hands on the desk. "More than alright, Laura, thank you," and Annie turned back to walk to her desk, a smile forming on her lips, her face brightening at the prospect of her writing career.

The next time Annie met with Allie on her college campus, the young woman related to Annie what was happening in her world. "How's your writing coming along," asked Annie, genuinely giving the young woman all the support she could.

"It's been going great!" Allie replied, more energized herself. "I got my first draft almost finished."

"What part are you having trouble on?" she asked, surprising herself with this rather bold question. She sipped her coffee with Allie across from her at the campus coffee shop. It's just the part with the love scene. I want to write a good one but don't know where to put it in a horror movie.

"Well, I'm no expert in horror films, but maybe you could have a monster creeping up on a couple, you know what I mean?" she chuckled a little inside.

"Oh yeah, I didn't think of that! Like when they're both stripped naked and a zombie comes in through the window..."

"You got it, Allie, just brainstorm. Jot notes down in your cell phone if you think of something during the day, or night. Ideas come when you least expect it." She steered clear of asking about any more details of her horror story, she just had lunch and it wouldn't go down that good.

Allie, thinking Annie would pressure her to start the rewrites, was surprised that Annie knew something that would perk Allie up and get her even more inspired.

"Now take a break for one day. Go ride your bike to meet friends. Give yourself a breather. Don't mention your script to anyone. Then the next day start your rewrites. Get relaxed and pat yourself on the shoulder for doing so well."

"I took your advice to put things down on the index cards," Allie said, shyly. To herself, Annie said, that's just how she is, nothing wrong with being a shy writer. "I might do some more last-minute rearrangements with my editing and plotline," she said, hands on her bike, that had stickers of emo and post-punk bands plastered on the front and back.

"And Allie? If you want me to read your screenplay after you've rewritten it until you're finished, I'd love to review it and comment on it," said Annie.

I'd like that," she said, looking off to one side, smiling back.

"You're doing so well, I can't wait to read it! shouted Annie. She realized later that was a promise she couldn't keep. She couldn't stand horror movies. Give me a romcom any day over that. Allie didn't need the feedback from her that bad. "Have fun with your day! Go enjoy yourself!" as Allie took off on her bike at full speed.

Chapter Twenty-six

JOSH
Why do you always cry
when I mention someone's
getting married?

KATE (wiping her eyes)
I…I don't know, maybe
I'm allergic to white
wedding gowns.

JOSH (joking)
That was a bad one.

KATE
Seriously, will I ever
stand at the altar? I
fantasize what I would be
wearing all the time. A
lovely lace midi dress?
Or should I dress in a
yellow robe with a
Buddhist theme?

JAKE

You're not serious? You
want to stand on a
mountaintop and be blessed
by the Dalai Llama? Not
that there's anything
wrong with the Dalai Llama.

KATE

Oh no, I want a lace gown.
Or maybe a poofy, marshmallow
gown.

JOSH

I heard you should always
go with your first choice.

It was a beautiful afternoon in Annie's favorite nature place, ten minutes from her home. Palisade Park. The writers and producers at Nine Figure Pictures were hosting a party in the park with many familiar faces. Couples and friends enjoyed each other's company. The old tree at the entrance of the park stood with its branches swayed by the continual movement of the cool breeze. There was a group of preteens enjoying their lunch in the park on the cool green lawn. Some were acting out, making the soft dance of the tree branches swirl higher. A grandmother from Peru sat watching her two grandchildren play hide and go seek.

She and Ian sat on the bench facing the water. They were both happier that things were turning out well with Nine Figure

Pictures. And they had their friendship.

After a pause, she shared, "I forgot to tell you! I've got good news! I had one of my screenplays optioned by a producer who knows Laura. She's really interested in my story."

"That's great," Ian said. It was clear he supported her advancement.

"And I quit wearing high heels. Bad for my feet. And no alcohol. It makes me depressed. This is our celebration!"

"Something I need to tell you," said Ian, slowly, measuring his words. "My supervisor liked my performance and work record at the office. They're keeping me on until I pass the bar."

"Oh good!" she smiled.

Carefully, Ian added, "About Piper and the wedding ... I don't want this to upset you ...."

"No, I'm so happy for you! Congratulations, Ian!" she interjected. Another pause.

"You're invited to the wedding, Annie."

"Are you sure that's a good idea?" She felt her heart drop.

"No, it's cool," said Ian.

"I'd love to! I'll be there!" She started to wipe tears from her eyes. Deep down, she didn't want him to marry Piper. She held her tears back. OK, don't lose your composure here. Even though it's hard, she thought.

"I shouldn't have told you," said Ian, opening his arms up for a hug, "Now you're upset....come here ..."

She accepted his embrace and laughed through her tears. "Ian, you almost broke my heart." She grabbed her purse and found a clean Kleenex, blowing her nose hard.

"What? Me? Annie, we're still friends. I hope you'll have a date to go with you. I can't see you coming to our wedding by yourself." "I'll think of someone," she said, genuinely interested in supporting her friend. .

A week later, she dragged herself to work. It was all she could do to make herself feel better. She sat at her desk, unwrapping a homemade sandwich, and ate in silence. Until coming by her cubicle was a familiar face with all smiles. It was Ogbay, who looked even more cheerful than he usually was, suddenly noticing Annie by herself. She was happy to see her friend.

Hey, Ogbay! How are you?" He chuckled. "Miss Annie Chen! How are you?" "Fine, Ogbay!" She continued, slyly under her breath. "How's your love life?" she chortled.

He sat down next to her. And announced, "I'm getting married! Next month!" he said with a big, equally sly grin on his face.

"Really! Congratulations!" Everyone is getting married! she thought hard to herself. When will my turn come, she pleaded, thoughts crowding her mind. "Speaking of weddings...Guess what? I'm invited to Ian's wedding," she said, but with a low note.

"*Really!*" He laughed. Then, sensing her frustration, he said, "Your turn will come. Just wait and see."

Chapter Twenty-seven

          KATE
Josh, I don't want you to
take this bad, but...

          JOSH(slowly)
Ye-e-e-s?

          KATE
I've got a proposal. A
marriage proposal.

She beams.

          JOSH(a bit shocked)
You? You what? Who is this
other guy?

         KATE(evading the question)
You were supposed to
congratulate me. You know,
since you're seeing that
other woman, Trudy
Trainwreck or whatever
her nickname is.

(pause)
**Weren't you planning on
marrying her?**

Next month, Annie told John she wanted to be at the wedding of
an old friend and told him she would love to have him there to
accompany her. John was obliging, but mostly because he wanted
to visit the wealthy part of L.A. for the first time. The location for
the wedding Ian and Piper picked was a charming spot at the
pricey Hollywood Hills Estate Garden for their wedding day. The
garden was made up of tiers of different species and colors of
roses. Ivory white banners were draped around the interior rooms
and more fresh roses in the adjoining dining hall dominated the
wedding theme.

A well-known cover band provided the music, with guests
already starting up the festivities before any reception, gyrating to
the rhythm guitar and rocking to the drumbeats. The lead singer
was wearing clothes that resembled the '80s with a torn top,
fishnet stockings and leather miniskirt, stomping around in boots,
belting out number one hits. Piper and Ian had scrimped and saved
the money to tie the knot there, or so it seemed.

That was the topic among a lot of the wedding guests. In truth,
Piper, with her job as a coat checker at a bar in Huntington Beach,
had literally bribed someone to keep the place free for three hours.
There was evidence of her using her feminine persuasion, or doing
some dirty work as favors, because she sure as hell didn't have

close the amount needed to rent the place from her menial job. Word got around about that, but everyone else was excited to be a part of the proceedings, maybe as an excuse to dress up and accentuate the illusion of being as important as your run-of-the mill movie star.

They were all talking to one another, with the standout in the crowd at her wedding award belonging to Piper. Her light brown hair done up in an attractive bun had cubic zirconia highlights set amongst an imitation baby's breath hair ornament when they reflected the sun. And that white gown, poofy though it was, intimidated Annie a bit with Piper being at the center of attention. The bride-to-be was chatting up a storm with Chuck, who wore a moustache and beard and looked like a Chippendale model from the '70s with his machismo shoulders and firm stomach. "You know, we look better than you and that guy again. What's his name?"

She raised her voice over the loud music. "It's Ian ... do you have a problem with that, Chuck?" She was slightly offended. Or that's how Annie read her face.

"What was that about?" Piper warned. "Where do you think all that stuff I gave you came from? From my salary? Why, we don't look compatible or something? You do know I'm getting hitched with him, don't you? Today, by the way," she said, with sarcasm. Then, seriously, "Doesn't he look handsome in his wedding shirt and slacks?"

Chuck just went along with her, not wanting to displease

anyone, especially not Piper. He got close to her so his breath was on her face. "Oh yeah, no I think that's great. I love….Uh ….Ian. Nice guy." He had just remembered his name. "Oh no, it's fine. Just haven't seen him for a long time. *You* look great," he said, nervously fidgeting with his drink. She must be kidding, Chuck thought, glancing over at Ian. What a nerd, he murmured, under his breath. Ian wasn't a nerd, Chuck just wanted to think of him that way. So he could feel more macho in comparison.

He reassured Piper. "No, you two are a happy couple, yeah, yeah," he said, wrapping his arms around her waist. Her indignation stayed on a few more minutes, but she got close to Chuck with the music playing and started to relax again. For one minute. After she saw the looks of Ian and another woman over his shoulder, talking and enjoying each other's company, Ian and, who was that? Talking like they had known each other for years…she kept staring at them. No one she knew. And she knew everyone he knew, so this was kind of strange.

And interesting, in a bad way. A really bad way, she thought, as she saw Ian's hand and arm go around this unknown lovely Asian woman's waistline, Annie with her shiny black hair. She wore a purple gown that set off her skin tone beautifully, with a graceful draped neckline that added sophistication to her demeanor.

Just at that moment, John stepped close to them, in a blue suit and formal white felt cowboy hat. "There you are!" as she gave him a hug. So happy we made it, John," said Annie. She took hold of his hand. "Ian, this is my friend, John." "Hey, thanks for making it here," said Ian, as he shook hands with John.

Ian led Annie a few feet away from John, and said, barely audible to anyone else, in her ear, "Yeahh...Annie, I really did mean all those things I said to you. When we were together. I still love our friendship."

"Really?" She wasn't sure about it, but it seemed to her he was telling the truth. "It's how I felt at the time. By the way, you look great."

Before she could react, Piper came up to them and tried to butt in. "Hey, who's this trying to steal my guy?" She started to take on a chilly demeanor, like an actress playing the part of a jilted gangster moll. Maybe it was the location that made her feel like a bad girl actress.

Ian, a little nervously said, "Piper, this is Annie."

Refusing to be defeated by this, Annie said, "He's all yours. Go tie the knot."

Everything was going fine, everyone in tip top condition, dressed to the nines. Mothers, fathers, their daughters and sons. They were there to show off their wealth, as parents of adult children who would never be able to afford attending this luxurious location on their own. Ian glanced at Chuck, and found something familiar about his suit and slacks. It looks like what I bought, the same colors and everything, he mulled over in his mind. Wait a minute, it *is* my suit and slacks...what the hell are they doing on *him*? He was about to bring it up with Chuck.

Utterly unprepared for what happened next, Piper's friend, Nelly, came up to her. She whispered in Piper's ear, then said, loudly over the music, "I hate to spoil your wedding day, but I notice your dress is turning a very bright shade of yellow."

Piper looked down at her dress in shock. She gave out a shout, "No, no!"

"Oh yes! And look at your underarms. You've got sweat stains. It happens at almost every wedding I go to. A white wedding turned into a lemon wedding," Nelly giggled, in spite of her friendship with Piper. Piper, aghast at this, looked down at her dress again.

"Oh, my god!!" she cried, starting to wail like a tortured duck. Ian, a bit amused, said, "You know, you do look like a lemon, in a way."

"Ohh, Ian!", she squealed.

"Honey, I'm just joking! I didn't notice anything. Did you dye your dress a nice shade of yellow instead of just going for the traditional white?" Piper simpered out loud and it sounded as if she were about to explode, with her low growling under her breath at this last remark.

One of the guests turned to Nelly and pointed out, "Oh, boy, here comes trouble. Don't move, just turn your head and pretend you're checking out the dessert bar." Nelly's eyes scanned the table, then her eyes widened, as a certain older man, dressed in a clean, crisp black and white suit and tie, looking like he was reincarnated from a wedding event from the 1960's, dived onto the table, grabbed the bowl of chocolate mousse, and licked his fingers and thumbs, until his hands were a complete mess. He eyed Piper, looking at her dress, then went up to her.

"Hey, sweetie, wanna dance?", not recognizing that she just might be the bride.

Piper recoiled, screaming, "Somebody, stop this guy!"

Nelly asked her man friend who this imposter was, and he replied, "That's why they call him Greasy Joe, always going after the food at weddings. I heard he even goes to memorial services, where he specializes in taking in deep fried drumsticks, anything greasy, like sausage and bacon at breakfast wedding buffets."

"What's a nice young lady doing here? Getting married to that guy? Join me for a dance?" He put his hands around her waist. Piper looked at her dress again, even more agitated.

"You crazy lunatic! What am I going to do? Look what you did! I'm a mess! Get away from me!" she recoiled in horror.

"I just couldn't resist. You look so purty!" Piper ran away from him, but Greasy Joe followed, chocolate-soaked hands and arms outstretched.

"Do you want a back massage?" he shouted, because his hearing was bad. Piper tried to keep herself out of reach of him, but he was rapidly gaining on her, so she grabbed ahold of Chuck and ducked behind him.

Ian, trying to regain order, said, "We'll just have to leave things the way they are. A little stain won't hurt." Piper composed herself, and came out from behind Chuck. The minister faced Piper and

Ian, as the couple stood together, silently. All of the guests watched, solemnly. "Remember that your life together may mean struggling for your happiness against all adversity. Now, if anyone has any reason to object to the matrimony between Ian MacDrew and Piper Wickham, let them speak now or forever hold their peace. Silence from the wedding guests.

No one dared say a word. They saw the tension between Ian and Piper, and even close friends said their relationship had changed. Distant and lacking in passion. It was as if all that finery and show of wealth didn't matter because where was the love? Things had gone lackluster over the few weeks of the wedding planning.

Except for the one that wasn't really invited. Greasy Joe stood up. "This little lady is too good for you, you young stud!" He grabbed her, hands smeared with melted chocolate, lifting her up in the air. Pretty strong for a little guy. Piper reacted, in shock, screaming. "Ohh!! No!!" Ian stood by, saying, "This old guy is high on the chocolate! What the…"

The minister said, "I take that as an objection?"

Annie watched, surprised. The guests also reacted, booing and shouting.

Piper entreated, "Our wedding! Ian!" Ian gave Piper a hug, trying to console her. But she couldn't stand it. "Ian, stop! You're ruining my dress!"

Two of the guests told Joe politely, that he would have to leave. John laughed. "Haha, I laughed when I saw what that old geezer was doin'. He put his designer touch to the bride's gown, both front and back!"

"You are really bad...You're not trying to get between them, are you? said Annie, raising her voice a bit.

"No, but a little action was needed for a serious hoedown like this one. And you did have the hots for the groom. I'm well aware o' that."

She was firm. "That's over now. We're just friends."

Ian marched up to her. "You planned this, didn't you? You wanted this to end in a complete disaster!"

She retorted, "What? I did not! I had no idea any of this would happen!"

"So that we could be together," he said, slowly and softly. Then, accusingly, he said, "I think you invited him to go after Piper's dress like that!"

Annie defended herself. "I'm completely innocent!"

"Yeah, you can be sure he is," a firm voice said. John was not amused. "I been with 'er the whole time and she never even met that greasy guy before."

Ian wasn't convinced. "And you were probably in on this, too."

"I claim my innocence and scout's honor on this one," said John, lifting his palms up in self-defense.

Ian started getting heated up. "You're lying!" Ian shouted. "Then *you* were the one who planned this whole thing to be a disaster! C'mon, tell me you did!"

"Ian, stop!" she cried. She was shocked at Ian's behavior, Ian who was always so calm and sensible.

John remained calm. "It's fine. I saw it comin'. He got that big ol'frown on his face from the beginnin'."

She tried to keep the peace between them. "Ian, he didn't do anything. And I swear, neither did I!"

Ian backed off. "Alright. But I know you were wishing it would all go wrong. And there wasn't going to be any wedding."

Before she could explain that wasn't her intention, Piper started to get hostile. "O.K. I'm calling this whole thing off. We're not officially married. Until things settle down." She turned to Ian, "I want to wait. I'm not ready to get married, anyway."

Ian wasn't convinced. "Great. What'll I tell your parents? And mine? That we're continuing to live in sin?"

Piper, repulsed, said, "You'll think of something. Meanwhile, I'm getting out of this, sweaty, stained, yechh, soaked, yechh, dress."

"And I'm going home," retorted Annie. "It was nice meeting you, Piper," she said, as she extended her hand for a shake.

As if it was even more nauseous to take her hand, Piper came back with, "Normally I would, but your hands just may be smeared with chocolate, and you smell like a dirty old man."

Then came the screams. A middle-aged woman, someone's mother who got invited to the wedding because she paid for part of the costs of the venue and her son and daughter's wardrobe, clutched at her handbag.

"Where is my credit card!" she rummaged through her bag. "It should have been here with my coat when I checked it in!" Her son tried to calm her down, to no avail, and slipped away to ask for a once over at the coat checker's booth near the park. No one was there at the time. She wasn't the only one who was in the raid. None of their credit cards were in any of the pockets of coats that the guests had left behind when the weather changed in the afternoon.

With all this chaos happening, Annie and John turned to leave and walk to his car. Guests left the park, dismayed by the half-baked wedding they were sure should have gone right.

Soon, another lady felt for her shoulder bag, and was also confused as to where the booth that was set up for the wedding was. Everyone seemed to be in a state of confusion at the occasion. Something was off. They had never attended a wedding like this one. "It was missing, just like the other lady!" she shouted, and other ladies began to look for their credit cards that were with them before the reception.

Annie's cell phone began to ring. "Go ahead to the car. I'll catch up with you later. I need to take this call," she said to John.

"Don't be long, sweetheart. We got traffic to beat," John reminded her.

Ian, sitting in a chair, was the only person who remained from the reception. He seemed oblivious to the chaos that ended what was expected to be a wonderful occasion. "Hello?" Annie said, as she answered her cell, frantically trying to get to the car.

"Annie. I miss you. You know you still mean something to me."

"Where's Piper? I thought you were with her …"

"Piper went home. She's taking a shower."

"You got to believe me, Ian. I didn't hijinx the wedding….."

He paused at this. "Alright." Changing his tone, he said, "I miss your hands on my body, Annie."   "But you have Piper. What about Piper's hands on your body?"

"Yeah, but you're different. O.K., I'll talk to you later."

He hung up as she tried to get through, "Ian? Ian! It's over between us. Don't you think you can …."

She heard him hang up. Sighing, she turned her phone off and ran to catch up and meet John.

Chapter Twenty-eight

The next week was difficult for Ian, and his only salvation was his work assisting lawyers and researching cases, meeting with clients and getting things ready for trials. At least it gave him some kind of hope for his future. Let's go to my favorite café, Brewbest in Hollywood, he told himself. I need to get away from relationships where no one knows me and just read.

He calmly drove his car in the direction of Sunset Boulevard. However, he soon discovered this spot was far from a refuge from his personal problems. He entered the cafe with feelings of being free, to have a whole table to himself. He positioned his backpack to pay the counterperson for a large chilled coffee, when he turned his head to see Piper. Yes, Piper.

But this time she was in heaven, her makeup looked spot-on, her body looking perfect in a dress and pearls, which he swore she never wore before,....and who the hell was sitting across from her? It was Chuck, her good old friend from the wedding. I ought to punch this guy's face in, right now! Messin' around with my fiancé.

Ian found a table to stake out as his own, when he noticed Chuck putting his hand in Piper's and whispering something in her ear that made her laugh. He leaned over to pick up a large duffle bag and pulled out a leather jacket. Wait, I wasn't able to find a jacket I lost like that one, last time I checked the closet. It looks like mine! In a few seconds he said to himself, that *is* the jacket I lost! Which one of them decided Chuck should have it? He draped the jacket over Piper's shoulders.

She was wearing a formal dress, not anything she could afford, and she never wore anything pretty like that when they were together. Not on her salary. And then, like no one knew anything at all about them, they actually kissed! A stolen kiss that was supposed to be saved for her future husband, me! thought Ian, as his spirits began to sink inside.

This was a blow that he did not expect. He wasn't going to be a party to this, no way. He turned to leave after gulping his caffeine down before he turned into a monster towards Chuck. He was deeply hurt by this lack of compassion in his so-called relationship with her, this lack of fidelity, but he supposed it was his karma coming back at him. Like the wind was punched out of him, he had to struggle to walk normally.

Finally reaching his apartment, he lay down with the pain inside. He didn't really like to face his reality, and all his energy was sapped, but something began to shift within him, too.

That evening when Piper returned home to the apartment she shared with Ian, she kicked off her heels and stomped through the door, walked past Ian in their living room and faced the window, not wanting to have eye contact with him.

He looked at her, frustrated in having no control over their relationship. "We've been together almost ten years now, Piper. You want to give up now?" She was unmoving, except to cross her arms tightly, staring out the window. She wouldn't dare look at him and honestly face him.

"We can't even get a decent wedding celebration to work between us. All I can say is things have changed between us. I don't know you as the same person anymore. We never have any fun together," she pouted.

"Whaddyou mean things have changed between us?!" he asked, not believing what he was hearing.

"I *mean*, it's not the same. There's no more feeling between us."

"Well, you know, relationships are like that, they go through ups and downs." He spoke with a small tremor. He had a feeling this would be happening. His first emotion that he had to admit to himself was fear. She turned to face him. "Ian, ever since our…our sad excuse for a wedding…your attention has been on other things. Like your law books. It's all you ever do, read your books!"

"But you know I've been trying to study to pass the bar. You know I've always wanted to be a lawyer. Defending disabled people who have no hope for themselves and can't always stick up for themselves…...the underage teenager forced to get involved with corrupt movie stars …." It just slipped past the radar. She couldn't have cared less.

"And I've found somebody else," she continued, as if the last sentence he said about his dreams coming true flew right past her.

"Someone who has time. That's all I ever wanted from you."

"But I needed some space for making my dreams come true. You told me that, remember? We made an agreement …."

Piper replied, flatly, "It just isn't working out. There's nothing going on between us. I'll be moving out starting tomorrow. Chuck found a nice temporary studio for me. And you know what? I'm going to make up for that lousy rehearsal of a wedding and invite three times more people, have a *huge* wedding cake, wear a *much* better wedding dress ……."

She turned to find him leaving, as he made straight for the door. He paused and looked behind him briefly. "Good luck, Piper. I wish the best for you."

Chapter Twenty-nine

                    KATE
    I found someone I really
    like. And you can get
    married now, in peace.

                    JOSH
    Yeah, yeah, I know. I want
    you to be happy!

                    KATE
    You'll have to meet him.
    He's like me, a writer.

                    JOSH
    Yeah, that's good. I can
    still come over. I mean,
    I'm not married yet.

                    KATE
    I hesitate on that one.
    No cheating!

Annie and John got out of the taxi as it pulled up to one of the few old but elite examples of high-end apartments in north Hollywood.

It was one of the Victorian painted ladies, restored to their original beauty. John must have a side gig to be able to afford this, she thought, on the day they had first been there together. Now they were planning to live there permanently. He opened up to her that his family came from a long line of oil drilling companies. They walked up the stairs, crossed the threshold and entered the sunny living room.

She sat down on the sofa, when John said, "Close your eyes. Now tell me what you think of this?" She closed her eyes. "My latest painting. Do you like it?"

Annie opened her eyes. "I love it!" It was a neo-abstract oil painting, not in her style of neo-realism, but she was still intrigued by it. "It's really joyful, and so....*red*...," she cocked her head, resting it on her hand, her other arm supporting it, trying to figure out what the painting meant to her. She wasn't an expert in modern art, but she was trying to be supportive as best as she could.

She settled in with John on his couch, which was worn out from nights sleeping on it after completing some of his paintings. He was "close to his work" and he took that as a serious but rather amusing saying put to good use.

"C'mon, sugar...why are you so serious," as he leaned over to peck her on the cheek. "I spent the past week staying up until 2 a.m. trying to finish these," he pointed to his paintings. At least he's devoted to his work. She had to hand it to him. She was just about to congratulate him on his painting again when John listened to his voicemail on his answering machine.

A sensual woman's voice with a strong Texas accent left a message for John.

"How ya'll doin' there, my sweet Texas man. This is your sugar, Vivian, remember me? Wasn't trying to be a sugar mama to you last time we met, but by gosh you know I am a cougar lady, remember?" Her voice trailed in an echo of sensuality with a baby-like accent, even at middle age.

"Who is that?" Annie demanded. "Shush! I'm listenin'!" as he leaned over to put his ear closer to the phone's answering machine.

"I've got plenty of gallery space for your new, wild paintings. I'll be comin' to California to pick them up. By the way, don't ya just miss my sexy Southern Belle body?"

He stopped the message, abruptly. "She's just some rich friend of my sister. She owns a gallery space in Texas. Someone from the past who has a crush on me, that's all."

Annie was too bright for that. "This is more than a crush!"

"That's all in the past, darlin'," he tried to reassure her.

"You know how much I need you, Annie. This woman, she just flirts with me because she loves my paintings." Annie tried to ignore this blatant expression of tooting his own horn.

"It's cold in here. Can I borrow a sweater? A boyfriend sweater!" She laughed to herself over that. John opened a chest of drawers. There was a small-sized ladies sweater with a low neckline in pink that he pulled out and threw at her." What's this? Where did you get this?" she asked, suspiciously.

"Oh, that's just an old sweater. Never could figure out how to get rid of it.

"You wear pink in ladies size small??" she asked. He ignored that comment, since there wasn't anything more he could do about it at that point. For her part, right then she just wanted time with him, even if it was only watching a late night movie. She pulled the sweater over herself and listened as John played back another message on his answering machine. "Just gotta give this a listen and I'll be *right* with ya."

"Hey, sugar...I'll be in California next week to see ya'll. I hope you ain't misbehavin' on me," said the woman's voice that had the same drawl as John.

"Who is this woman?" Annie demanded, again.

"Oh, she's just an ol' friend o' the clan from Texas. I told ya, it's nothing to worry about, she's that way with everyone. She's just some jailbait from the past trying to get her way with me," he said, untruthfully. Honestly, she was the one older than him. "I don't know how she got into the art gallery business." She wasn't convinced.

In an effort to make her feel better, or maybe he had other shady reasons, John opened the drawer of a small table near the couch. "That's nothin'. Here's somethin' for ya," he said, trying to calm her.

He took out a small red jewelry box from his drawer, knelt down on one knee to her and opened it to display a small, gold banded diamond ring.

Naively, she opened her mouth in disbelief and took in a quick breath, which she held for a few seconds.

"This lil' ol' rock is for you. Will you marry me, Annie?" Her expression changed from skepticism to one of ecstasy.

"Really?? For *me*?" she replied. "Of course I will marry you!" She kissed and embraced him.

"Save that for later, sweetpea. Now we gotta plan our weddin' day," he said, pulling back and relaxing on the couch.

She was overjoyed. And did a real happy dance this time around.

Chapter Thirty

>   JOSH
> This dating other people
> idea. I don't think it
> was such a good idea.

>   KATE
> But that's because I stopped
> taking action looking for
> someone. I just had to keep
> at it.

>   JOSH
> Hey Kate, talk to you later.
> My exam is coming up. I
> have to hit the books and
> study.

>   KATE
> Alright, alright, just
> trying to help.

Annie had to share this with Ian, and still be friends with him.

They made that promise to each other, to stay friends always. It was a day where sunlight filtered through the trees surrounding the house Ian was living in. Larger than the rented dwelling he lived in before. Still in Santa Monica but in more comfortable surroundings, he was still based there on assignment where he worked at the law firm.

She took in the atmosphere. She was going to let him know and he would be happy for her. Knocking on his door, a bit cautiously, she took a few steps back to show she wasn't too eager to see him. After a few more knocks, Ian opened the door to see her. "How are you, Ian?" She tried to say it carefully. She felt refreshed, taking in his familiar face. "Hope you don't mind me stopping by."

"Hey, I'm renting this new place. I wanted you to come see me. I got your call."

"This place is wonderful, Ian." After a pause when they felt that reconnection between them, she was curious.

"What about Piper? Aren't you with her?"

He took a breath in. "Piper and I aren't together anymore, Annie. I'm alone now." He said it woodenly, as if feeling the loss and the loneliness.

"Really?" she asked, not believing what she had just heard.

"We're not getting married. Piper is seeing someone. Another man."

Annie had trouble taking this in. "She was seeing someone around the time we met, and even flirted with him during what you saw was a disaster and a lame attempt at a wedding."

"Ian, you don't have to go into detail. I'm shocked that she did that to you," she added, figuring she needed to offer her perspective about the situation they were all in. Annie just couldn't help asking, "Is she happy with him?" Then she answered her own question. "I guess she must be, after doing all that."

She hesitated before this, with a voice trying to be calm. They looked at each other quietly. Surprised at himself that he forgot to tell her the news, he motioned with his hand for her to come inside.

"I'll stay for a little…" She walked into the spacious, rustic living room where she felt the quiet atmosphere. It felt so calm and relaxed. A perfect respite for her life that was getting to be so busy, too hectic for her all at once. For a few seconds she felt really safe there.

He slowly and carefully eyed the coffee table near the couch, where a well-worn local newspaper covered Ian's books. Some familiar faces she recognized stared up at them, in the front page news. The headline shouted, Bride Fakes Her Own Wedding with Massive Credit Card Fraud. The color photos of Piper and Chuck, their faces gaunt and expressionless, almost seemed to pop off the page, their eyes staring at the camera in a police lineup presenting their name, height and weight, and the dates of the photos. Annie's mouth dropped, and she took a long, audible breath in.

"Yup, I know," began Ian. They sat down, Ian in his comfy chair and Annie on the couch.

"This is beyond anything I could even imagine, Ian…"

"Piper didn't want to see me again. It got to the point where she was stealing my clothes so that she could have her boyfriend in them," he said, looking at the floor. Can you imagine that, Annie?" he said as he shook his head. "And all those people at the wedding. She had accomplices working with her and Chuck. Positioned right in the outdoor coat check stand. Credit card fraud...what next?" He swiped his hair back and leaned his head on his hands. "Now I know why my dad never liked her."

They took a few minutes just to process their emotions. They were both feeling foolish that they were misled like that. "These two criminals were busted," he declared. He said it in a way he would never have described Piper. The Piper he knew. But he realized she was only using him at this point.

"Yes, they were, and you deserve so much better." She tried to calm him down with her words, softening her tone.

"That was why Piper was overjoyed I found a job out-of-town, so she wouldn't get caught stealing with her boyfriend."

Annie shook her head, and sighed. "She conned us, all along, they both did," and couldn't think of anything else to say to try and make him feel better.

After a moment, but still trying to accept his reality, Ian asked, "What are you doing tonight, Annie? Let's go out for dinner. That Indian restaurant ... the one we first went to."

It was hard for her to say, "No, I'm with John now. I don't want to go against him on that.

"Yeah, O.K." Ian turned to go back into the house. But he wasn't going anywhere. He went to the kitchen and took out two bottles of sparkling water, one of which he gave to her. She didn't expect him to say anything. "Hey. I was thinking," he spoke, suddenly. "Would you and John mind if we all go out?" A pause.

She felt something here. She felt safe about it. "No, we wouldn't mind." Annie surprised herself with her reply.

"O.K., meet me at the restaurant," he said, eagerly. "I'll see you then. Friends as always," she said with a smile.

Chapter Thirty-one

At the Indian restaurant, Hollywood Curry, where they both loved the food, Annie waited for both John and Ian to show up. As Ian walked up to the front doors, he was close enough to see John, who was speaking to a young, attractive woman wearing a tight-fitting thigh high short dress, leaning on a bicycle. She could have been a young college student. Ian watched in dismay as he kissed her passionately and hugged her. "I'll see you later, at my place!" she said. John agreed, and went back into the restaurant to sit next to his wife-to-be.

Ian sat across from John and an unsuspecting Annie, who was looking intently at the dinner menu, side by side with John at the booth. This time Ian was civil. He reached out to shake John's hand. "Hey man, how ya doin'." He somehow found the words to say this, even after the startling discovery. "Alright," said John.

Ian felt it important to say this. "About the wedding. I apologize for accusing you," he said, head lowered a bit.

"I don't even remember it," John replied. "Now that you reminded me, I was thinking, you yankees sure know how to give a warm welcome to us southerners," he said, chuckling.

To Annie, Ian said with a little smile, "So this is where I said, "I have a girl...I could so fall in love with you..."She laughed quietly.

John was skeptical. "I'd be out of that relationship in a minute. Love triangles? It's not my thing."

"Well I didn't know about Piper until later. I straightened out after Ian told me he was engaged," she said, squirming in her seat. To avoid an awkward moment that could have happened, she took out a painting from her shoulder bag that she had finished, of Ian's cat, MacGregor. "Oh, before I forget...here's the painting. You can still give it to Piper. But he *is* your cat."

Ian stared at it, taking in the details up close. "It's beautiful." John agreed, "A work of art, darlin'." After another close look at the painting, he made his decision. "I'm keeping it", said Ian. "For me." He put it aside and gazed at her sweet face. She hoped it was a good ice breaker.

But then John brought up some uncomfortable experiences. Experiences Annie didn't want to hear or for Ian to hear, either. But John couldn't be stopped. "The last woman I dated took me home. And her husband was there fast asleep. We were really quiet about it." Annie cautioned him, "Maybe we better stay off the subject of dating." She gave him a serious look, hoping he heard her.

Apparently not. "I could tell you a few stories," he burst out laughing, completely ignoring her comments. Annie and Ian stared at him, silently. "O.K. I met a woman at a cougar party," John continued.

"You mean, me?" she said, hopefully.

"No, it was before that. I said to her, 'Hey, sugar, you're hot. Come back to my place.' I find out later, she's a man with a sex change." He laughed loudly. Some of the customers in the other booth turned to stare at him.

"You're lying. Really?" she said, embarrassed. John was still laughing. "He was attractive as a woman!" He paused. "Cougar parties and conventions are good places to meet people. No commitments, no nothin'."

"I thought you were looking for a long-term relationship, John," said Annie, puzzled. "Yeah, but it depends. You're the exception." She smiled again, momentarily reassured. Ian, however, was fidgeting in his seat, pressing his foot under the table on hers and spoke to her under his breath, while John went to the counter to order a beer.

"Annie? Can you come here for a minute? Annie, I want to talk to you in private. Come here."

"What, what's this about?" she asked, confused.

He stood up and took her hand to lead her to another table, out of earshot from John.

"OK, I know this is going to be hard to hear, but John is just using you. I need to tell you something ..." He explained what he saw before John entered the restaurant.

She didn't want to believe it. "What?! He just proposed to me, last night!"

"Annie, he's not the right guy for you. I hate to see you fall for that kind of guy. I know the way they are. They can't settle down with one woman. I don't want you to waste time with him."

"You're the one who said, 'Be a forceful Ox lady and get over here,' when you wanted me to go over to your place. And you were dating Piper when you met me. You were living with her! Do you really think you're better?"

"I was just flirting with you. I didn't expect us to take our relationship seriously at first. All I can say is I don't want you to be with him."

"Stop telling me what to do!" she whispered, loudly. Annie cut through what he was telling her. Some of the other customers peered over at them, especially at Annie, who was clearly out of sorts with all that was happening to her world.

John, in a good mood with his beer in hand, noticed the two of them talking. "There's the future little woman of my life! Are you tryin' to steal her away from me, or what?" he said, only half in jest.

Ian abruptly stood up. He knew what he couldn't change. "Alright, I gotta go. See ya later," he said as he walked towards the doors, his back hunched over and feeling humiliated.

She angrily laid in on John, "Look what you made him do. He's feeling bad because of all the awful things you were talking about!" John tried to stop her and pulled her close to him.

"Yeah, but you're in love with me, hon, don't you remember? He'll go back to his woman, don't worry, sugar."

"No, he's not going to. Piper's already seeing another man," she said, flatly.

"Well, glory be to God on that one," he answered. "She was too fast for him. He'll find his way. Now let's go home to have a little fun, Texas style." They stood up to leave, while John put his arm around her shoulder.

She stopped for a bit until he said, "C'mon, sugar, let's go!" impatiently. John steered her away from Ian as he was leaving, but Annie caught a glimpse of him out of the corner of her eye. She felt his hurt, as he took his hands out from his jeans and made his way to his car.

Chapter Thirty-two

In the early morning haze, Ian was at his desk, engrossed in his law books, flipping pages, reading intensely, putting his eyes close to the book. A ring on his phone enlivened the deadness of his surroundings in the old house, a perfect place for him to not be bothered by the world, and his aspirations to pass the bar were determined by his steadfast faith in study.

"Hello?" Who could be calling him? His only friends now were his co-workers, and even that was shrouded in superficial benign talk of gossip, people waiting for a promotion. Within the past couple of months, things changed at work for him. He had popped in at work and passed by his friend Andy, another law clerk who sat in the next cubicle near his office. "Hey, I just wanted to share the news. I got promoted today."

"Alright, man, cool!" said Andy.

"This means I have more duties assisting the lawyers and meeting with clients. I finally got that second raise I've been dreaming of," he cheerfully told his workmate.

"That's great, Ian," he remarked. "Not many can achieve that." But his voice went monotone as he relayed his congratulations. Andy was hoping for his own promotion and position as a lawyer, and Ian had beat him to it. They were always civil to each other, not overly friendly, but now Ian could feel the chilliness in his co-worker's voice.

It could all change in a day's work. People who you were friendly with would all of a sudden turn into rivals. But surprisingly, that was exactly the attitude he loved. He thrived on the friendly, healthy competition. He did want to get back that camaraderie he used to have with Andy. Maybe I should treat him to lunch, he turned over in his mind, as the phone call made him jump. He couldn't imagine who it was.

"Hi Ian. Can I come by later today? I just wanted to see you." Her familiar voice caught his attention. "Haven't been able to talk to you in awhile." Ian could have easily said no, and push away any human contact besides his workmates, but he was interested in Annie. "I love our friendship," he remembered he had told Annie, after the first few weeks of dating her.

A half hour later after arriving home from work, Ian opened the heavy oak door and saw Annie, looking radiant and standing near the doorway. Ian was genuinely happy to see her again.

"I wanted to tell you, my screenplay producer, Barbara, told me she sold my screenplay, 'Karma,' to Laura. They gave the green light to the project and it will be in production next year!"

she said, with a big happy smile at him. She wanted to have dinner with him just so they would celebrate.

He smiled, wearily. "No, Annie, I'm happy for you, but I can't. I've got to prepare for my class. I gotta study. But I'm glad you thought of me."

"Well, if you change your mind about dinner let me know," she said, sincerely. He shook his head. "I hate to say no, but I really better study. The bar exam is in a few weeks and I still need to wrap it up with my business law class. It's what I've been working on for a long time now." He stood in the doorway, not moving.

"I understand." She backed off, then turned away. Before she forgot, she turned back once to say, beaming at him, "Good luck on the exam." She waved, and respectfully took off in her car.

The next week found Annie meeting with her parents. There was something to discuss about her new husband-to-be. Annie's dad made clear his opinion on Annie's dating. When he heard that she was planning on marrying John, he urged her to visit with him and share a few words. She was happy to oblige, and was certain her father was going to offer words of praise and congratulations. He must be eager to meet John. Her dad hardly ever asked her to stop by to discuss her dating life.

Contrary to this, she didn't expect his reaction to her proposal to be anything other than praise and goodwill wishes.

"Why do you have to settle down with him," said her dad. "Those guys from Texas are really kind of macho, you know. Why can't you find a nice Chinese student? They're plenty of them near the university."

Annie stifled a laugh. She didn't want to put down her dad in any way, but the thought of her settling for someone else amused her. She knew they cared, and she loved both of them, even if they weren't seeing eye to eye with her. And it was true that John was a far cry from what they were familiar with.

Her mother began trimming the plants in their home, a modest one-story house that they had paid for with her dad's salary as a professor and her own as a doctor. She stopped for awhile to get through to her daughter.

"Annie, you do remember I worked hours taking care of the patients at the clinic, since you were a child, just to raise you in comfortable surroundings. Maybe you were too young to remember."

Annie glanced at her mother's collection of Asian art in the form of jade carvings and Chinese embroidered cushions. She did know that part of their salary went into collecting those things that her parents loved and reflected their culture.

"Oh, shush, Daddy. You know she won't listen to you. Always has to go against people." She focused on Annie. "Now, Annie, why don't you find yourself someone more educated?"

Annie pursed her lips and furrowed her brow, obstinately. "I'm not trying to go against you two," she interjected. "He comes from a good family. They have ties with Texas oil companies."

"I still don't like him," interjected her dad, stubbornly. His remark brought back memories of John's surprise visit to meet her parents.

"Well now, this is a quaint little Chinese home you have here," John had said, aiming to please her mother. "I've been in Chinese houses before but you really got it down, from this expensive-looking furniture to this sofa here. How much did you pay for all of this? Must be a fortune." Annie's mother responded, quickly.

"You have the nerve to ask me how much it cost to make our home presentable to visitors. I will say one thing, our family worked hard to do this. We didn't come with silver spoons in our mouths." I worked hard for my pay at the hospital, and my husband as a professor."

John didn't know better than to argue with her. It wasn't until later that Annie found out he had wealthy parents who profited from oil fields in Texas. It was the only way he survived as an artist. Maybe John was hoping to profit even more in his marriage prospects?

"Whoa, hold on, Mrs. Chen," he said, in an effort to calm her down, and maybe to try to take back what he said. "I just was telling y'all, it looks like you all come from *money*. That's all. You're too sensitive or something. Boy, what I got into, I don't know." He had a way of saying how he felt without worrying about the reactions he got from it.

Snap to the present. Annie's mother took control. "Let me tell her." She sat down close to Annie and looked straight into her eyes. Her dad was always more aloof when he was mad, but her mother was more straightforward, but gentle.

"Annie, you don't want all his friends to come over. You know you can't stand watching people use those horses. Just for entertainment. You know what they do to those poor animals after they're too old to buck with those cowboys. We know you, Annie, and you're an animal activist inside. And also, do you expect to have him eating out with us at the nice Chinese restaurants? He probably isn't used to it."

Her father agreed. "Listen to Mommy. He won't ever eat dim sum with us when he would rather ride a...a...whatchamacallit, a bucking bronco. I bet he wouldn't even remove his hat when he's with us, like at a wedding."

"Dad, that's a stereotype!" She paused to rethink what she just said. "Well, maybe not exactly." She remembered how John always ordered hamburgers at restaurants and his craving for steaks and potatoes when eating at upscale restaurants they saved up to go to. "O.K., I'm not listening to this," she said, quickly but stubbornly. "John and I are staying together and we'll be married, no matter what!" Somehow, as much as she loved both of her parents, she realized they may never accept anyone she dated, much less get married to. It wouldn't matter, because their family ties were strong. There was still a lot of love there.

She should have been mentally prepared for this, since she knew her parents' reactions to things involving relationships, most of all. It was the last thing she wanted to do, to be at opposite ends to her parents. She calmed herself down.

"Don't worry, Mom, it's really OK. John is a decent man. He's an artist, like me. I know you'll get used to him." It seemed like it was the best thing to do, just to put her parents at ease about the wedding plans. She was feeling it herself and her family was just a reflection of that.

Chapter Thirty-three

Vivian, a vivacious and curly-headed blonde southern belle with a mind for modern art, arrived at the airport with a pink suitcase in hand. She was carrying on the family business of art gallery shows, and her steady stream of wealth from the old money of Dallas, Texas showed with her style of dress, as explicit as it hinted to be. Her only curse, or blessing depending on how you took it, was she was sexy as hell. And she flaunted it like a movie star.

She hailed down a cab in her hot pink dress with lots of exposure. "Where you headed to, sweetheart?" the taxi driver flirted.

"Just where I want to be, in north Hollywood." "You sure lookin' pretty," the driver kept saying.

"I'm savin' myself for someone special, now you just stop," interjected Vivian, even though it was obvious she loved the attention. "Now here's the address I'm going to. I have a very important mission to accomplish." They arrived in half an hour as Vivian took the keys she had to enter John's house. In order to give him fair warning, she called on her cell.

"Hi, sugar. Couldn't wait. I took a shortcut. I got a taxi from the airport. I'm right outside your door now. Honeybun." Not hearing an answer on the phone, she took out a pair of keys from her bag and entered his place, rushed to the bathroom, undressed and turned on the shower.

Just at that moment, Annie entered the house and told John she wanted to freshen up. "Aren't you gonna change into that sexy outfit for me?" said John as he threw a see-through nightgown that showed off the wearer's thighs at her.

A little put off, but trying to make John happy, she took the nightgown in hand and opened the bathroom door. She screamed when she discovered Vivian, who was getting dressed in nothing but a towel after taking her shower.

"What are you....*who* are you!" Annie dropped the nightgown on the floor. She came out to confront John. "Who? Who is this?! In your bathroom?!" an exasperated Annie demanded.

John mumbled under his breath to himself, "Damn! She wasn't fast enough!"

"Oh, her?" he calmly answered Annie. "Oh that must be my sister's friend. The one who's renting her spare room. That lady who owns the art gallery. Darn, honey, I thought I told her we were comin' over."

Vivian, now dressed in a black minidress showing plenty of

cleavage and backside, said, trying to calm Annie, "Hi, darlin'. It's me, Vivian. I heard so much about ya."

Annie was still reeling. "You're John's sister's friend?"she said, incredulously. It was clear when she was exasperated and mad. "I thought she was meeting you at the airport."

"I took a shortcut, honey. Wanted to surprise my special man."

"OK. It's obvious there's something going on here!" cried Annie, backing off from both of them. But she stood her ground.

Vivian was nothing but amused, "Where did you meet this woman? My sweet beJesus, ya'll know how to pick'em up."

Annie wouldn't let up. She held her palms up, hoping for a good enough answer from her future husband. "John. You said she was just a friend!"

"She *is* just a friend," John retorted. "Aren't you, darlin'?" Vivian embraced John.

"Oh, yeah, just an ol' buddy o' mine, sugar." John pushed Vivian away. Even he was slightly put-off.

To Annie, John turned and said, "Annie, I promise this craziness will end." Then he turned back to Vivian, who was fluffing her hair to make it look poofy. "Why don't you let me drive you to Kate's place."

As if Vivian didn't hear, he whispered to Annie, "I'm takin' her over to my sister's. Now. She's gettin' overheated." Annie wasn't convinced. Accusingly, she aimed at John. Without letting up. "You said there was nothing between you and her. That better be the truth."

"I'll be back before you can say 'Chicken Fried Corndog'," said John, with no hesitation in his voice. He opened the door quickly and took off with Vivian.

Annie didn't wait for his return. She got into her car and directed it towards her best friend's rental. Another fine day of endless summer shadows and sun filtered through the trees, bouncing off the front door of Ian's house. She was determined to keep her friendship with Ian. Maybe he would be in a better mood today, she ruminated.

Ian looked at his reflection in the mirror. His eyes had slightly more sags with dark shadows under them now, from all of his studying. A knock on the door. It was Annie again, standing and waiting patiently at the door.

Honestly, Ian was actually feeling better and welcomed the much-needed break from all of his law books. "Hey! What's up?" he said, eager for the company and grateful that Annie thought about him.

"Can I come in?" That was the bold initiative Annie always seemed to have. He really loved that about her. She was still so attracted to him. As a friend, of course. "I just came by. I won't be long. Just to tell you. I'm going through with it. I'm getting married in a few days. For sure this time. To John." She was proud of herself that she was embarking on a full-fledged, long-term relationship with someone. It certainly wasn't a four or five night stand.

Ian looked disappointed and turned away. He managed to let

out a few words. "That's great." He didn't really feel great, mostly from these words that Annie had to let him know.

"Congratulations. Annie, you're with John now. Why did you even bother to see me?" He was struck by this and was tumbling downwards.

"Ian, we're like family. You don't have to feel ashamed about all of this. I'm happy."

"I know, but you have to be faithful to John. You shouldn't have bothered to come here. Why are you tempting me like this?" he asked, bitterly.

"I'm so proud of you, Ian. You've become who you wanted to be …"

Ian, protective of his feelings, abruptly said, "I have to study, Annie. My exam is in a few days. I'm expecting my professor to call because I had a question about the test materials. I really can't talk now. But thanks for stopping by."

"O.K., I'll talk to you soon," she said, her own voice faltering. But remember, you'll always be someone special to me." She reached forward and gave him a tight hug. "Alright. Later," he managed to say, while pulling back. He didn't need this now, it crushed his soul. He turned to go, then turned back again to Annie. "Hey, have a great wedding." She smiled. At least she got his well wishes, or so she thought.

At John's place, Annie felt cozy with her husband-to-be. She was hoping the wedding would go without a hitch and it would be perfect. Or approaching perfection, maybe. She sat in an armchair where she frantically wrote down notes in a folder, and stopped to check with John. "I think we got all of our friends to come to our wedding."

John, a little distracted, obliged, "That'll be fine." With a few clicks on her laptop, she said. "OK. I sent out the invitations a few days ago. Let's see how many can make it." Emails popped up everywhere. "Great! Everyone's RSVP'ed back and said they can be there! I am so looking forward to this."

Someone pounded at the door. John got up to answer it. "Who is it?" Annie asked, frantically.

Vivian, determined to get in, answered to John, and ignored Annie. "Hon, I forgot my shirt from last time. I left it there in the closet."

"Sure darlin," he smiled, "…anytime." As he let her come in, she made a beeline to the bedroom closet and frantically looked through all of the clothing. After about a half hour of digging around, she finally gave up on that. Annie stared at her, speechless. Even a little amused.

"Oh, darn. Can't find it." Her eyes darted to Annie and John. "I feel as embarrassed as a 'possom without his prickles on a June day...oh, that looks like my shirt." She pointed at the blue oversized shirt that Annie was wearing.

"No, that's mine," Annie defended herself, quickly. Vivian started to resist Annie's boundaries. She tugged at the shirt.

"That's mine, honeybunch. I can tell. I wear size 10."

Annie wouldn't give in. "It's size 10 but I know what my

clothes look like," she said, offended. "I like the loose look anyway, not like you," hoping she would leave soon.

"I remember now, John, you let me borrow this," Annie said, confused at the mix-up. "So it's hers?"

"Oh no. It's my sister's. She let Vivian wear it." Fed up with the whole mixup, Annie left the room to change the shirt to one she knew was hers.

As she came out again, Vivian was in a heated discussion with John. "Fiance?! John, you never told me...!"

"We're getting' hitched. It's less than 48 hours away," he said, decisively.

Finally, she announced, "Alright. I'll just go my merry way. And leave you two turtledoves alone," she said with a hint of disappointment.

"O.K. Here," Annie extended her hand for a handshake while thrusting the shirt at Vivian. "This is yours. I don't know what you mean by 'last time', but I think I can sense it. Goodbye and it was nice to meet you." Vivian ignored the hand gesture and turned to leave. "But if it doesn't work out, call me, sugar, anytime," she added, turning back to look at John. John opened the door for her.

"Thanks, darlin'. Nice to have some good ol' Texas sunshine in here. Thanks for bringin' it with ya."

"Anytime, turtledove!" She peeked in for a last look at John as he closed the door.

He turned back to Annie, who took a big breath of air and continued, as if nothing had happened.

"O.K. So this is how I want our wedding...", but he didn't know the anguish she felt inside. She wanted the wedding to be the best ever, and not end up a failure like Ian and Piper's wedding plans. Who are you kidding, she said to herself. This woman is not letting go! Can't she take a hint?

"I'm going for a drive. It's getting uncomfortable here." She got in her car, she just needed to get away. This wasn't going like she had planned. For months she had been anticipating the happiness that this big day would bring.

Driving up to Palisades Park on her own, she parked in the lot near the hiking path. Then she even surprised herself, taking out a bottle of beer she had hidden in the glove compartment. No cops around here, she reassured herself. She chugged it down and tossed it in the recycling bin. My life is starting to go downhill. I've got to get a grip on myself.

That is the last bottle of alcohol I am going to have, she said, out loud with determination. Well at least the last I drink before driving…

Then the thought surged from within her. I'm not going to let anyone get in the way of my plans for this wedding. I've got to face this on my own. She took a deep breath in and drove to the garden in Palisades Park outside the Victoria Building, a historical landmark where the wedding would take place.

It was the perfect setting for a June wedding. A beautiful sunset greeted her, and the flowers had a sweet scent that added to the romantic sight.

As she drove home, she vowed she wouldn't let her own negativity get in the way of hers and others' happiness.

Chapter Thirty-four

On the day of the wedding, a row of Annie's two nieces and two nephews were dressed in light blue charming chiffon dresses, with white shirts and light blue bowties for her nephews. Annie was excited and in high spirits.

Smiling, she addressed her mother, who it seems, was still not crazy that her daughter would be marrying "a bothersome redneck from Texas who faked that he liked Chinese food." Annie thought she would eventually get over her resistance to him being her son-in-law after the wedding.

"Mom, thanks for being here. I knew you would come around about all this," while planting a kiss on her mother's cheek.

"Whatever will make you happy. You're all grown up now, I can't tell you what to do," she said, gesturing with her hands to swipe away any notion to try to change her daughter's decision. Whatever her daughter wanted to do. But in the back of her mind she was still fighting off thoughts of how awkward any future family get-togethers might be.

Annie flung her head back and tamed a tendril of hair coming loose from the upsweep of her elegant hairdo, when she noticed Vivian was present, standing away from the others, wearing a bright magenta minidress with strap exposures along her belly and above her behind, that showed plenty of naked back and cleavage in the front. She overheard Vivian and John speaking to each other.

"Honey, if you're gettin' the weddin' jitters, you can call this whole thang off if you want to," said Vivian, her voice still audible despite her trying to lower her voice." She paused as she put her hands on the back of John's neck and said, voice as low as she could in his ear, "Nothin' is keepin' you. You don't really want to wed that China doll…do ya?"

Annie took note of that comment. By her expression, she took offense to it. Shaking her head, she listened to John's response.

"C'mon, Vivian. You're spoilin' my weddin' day," John replied, shaking her off of him.

"No, you need a real Texas sweetheart with a big Southern belle heart to match," she continued, louder, as Annie walked over to them. She took baby steps because on that one occasion she allowed herself to wear white satin kitten heels. Stumbling over herself, she came up to where John was standing.

She addressed him, quietly, "You aren't having second thoughts about this, are you, John?"

John, not desiring that any decent looking female in his world would take their attention away from him, he replied, "Me?? No, you just bet your little ol' be-a-u-tiful body we're gettin' married like we all planned. Come hell or swampwater," as he awkwardly pulled Annie to him by his side and steered her towards the front of the main hall of the Victorian.

There were about sixty guests as John and Annie took their places where the minister stood. He promptly began the service. "Ahem," he cleared his throat, "We are gathered here today to celebrate the wedding of Annie Chen and John Fitch ..."

Vivian, standing in the far back behind all of the guests, brushed her hair and applied another coat of makeup to her face, staring into her pocket mirror. She adjusted her breasts placement and took a good long look at herself, swaying from front to back, admiring what she thought was her sex appeal.

"O.K., sugar," she said to her best friend, which was her own self in the mirror, "Work that Southern belle magic here. Ya'll are not slippin' through my fingers ..."

The minister continued the ceremony as Vivian stood at the doorway's entrance at the back of the main hall and fixed her gaze on John.

Annie looked at John, also, then at the minister, starting to feel stuck, solemnly staring in front of her.

"If anyone should have any reason to object to the union of this couple," the minister said calmly, "John Fitch and Annie Chen, speak now or forever hold..."

"Stop!! John!" Vivian leaped from the back of the room and ran up to the couple, who stared in disbelief over what was happening. "You're the real love o' my life and you will always be! So get your paws off that woman and marry me!"

Just then and there, Annie knew what to do. She pulled the wedding ring off of her finger, opened Vivian's eager palm and put the ring in it. "You're the best one for him, sweetie. I just couldn't give him the love he deserves. Have fun at your hoedown, sugar!" she said, smiling, and loud enough to let it be known to the large gathering of confused guests.

Vivian took the ring and gave it to John. *Annie* took this opportunity to release her aching feet from the tiny heels, run from the main hall and crossed the doorway, holding up her poofy white gown and fleeing from the wedding scene in her bare feet, heels dangling from her fingers.

Meanwhile, the minister cleared his throat and adjusted his speech. A bit surprised, he began again, "Uhh, we are gathered here today to celebrate the union of John Fitch and..." "Vivian Fraser," she stated, as John slid the oversized diamond rock onto her finger.

By this time, Annie frantically searched for her car in the parking area, with passersbys staring and muttering to themselves. "Hey lady, are you running away from your wedding?" a curious-looking man asked. Annie replied, firmly, "I'm making the best decision I've ever made! And I feel *great* about it!"

Revving up her car's motor, she headed towards Oceanview

Park, and when she arrived, lifting her dress, stumbled quickly down the sun splattered walkway, the palm trees swaying in the light breeze. The broad view of the Pacific Ocean was beautiful that day, sparkling water around views of the blue mountains in the distance. The morning shadows fell lightly from the golden sun onto the sidewalk.

Having enough of the heels, she whipped them off her hands and flung them into the sand, running through the shimmering park path towards where she knew Ian would be. It was his favorite spot in the world, as well.

Sitting under a shady tree, he peacefully looked at his law book. He had no doubt he would pass the bar, but couldn't ignore the pangs of loneliness that accompanied his mood that day, when his best friend was getting married. At that moment, he decided to call it a day. Putting his book away in his shoulder bag, he looked around to see if he left anything, and glanced up with disbelief at Annie, who was running towards him in that poofy, chiffon wedding dress, that she decided made her look like a meringue puff.

"Ian! I didn't marry John! You were right. He was never faithful to me!" Ian threw his bag aside. Annie, breathless, plopped herself like a deflated marshmallow onto the warm grass in front of Ian.

"I told you so. I was trying to warn you." Still reeling from the surprise of seeing her again, he told her, "You never said how you felt about me."

"You were engaged. Are you still bitter about Piper?"

"No," he said, as he stretched his arms, tired of hunching over his book. "It wasn't meant to be." He didn't want to talk about Piper anymore. He just wanted to be with Annie.

And Annie, at that point, made the realization she was cured. She wasn't a casual dating game player, a jaded 'other woman' she thought she was before, or others thought she was. She wasn't second best. She was first. She just made up her mind.

They drew closer to each other, feeling the familiarity of a strong hug. His scent of forest pine drew her towards him. It fit him naturally, not the overdone fragrance of any other man. He drew back, to look into her eyes.

"Annie Chen," he paused, taking a deep breath, "will you marry me, and be Annie Chen McDrew?"

She moved closer and gave him another enormous hug. "Yes, Ian McDrew," she said, "from the future Annie Chen McDrew." He chuckled, and Ian and Annie smiled. Content.

"Just think, Annie," as he rocked her in his arms, "You'll have this every night from now on."

"And that's how I like it," she said, as they kissed and held each other in an embrace, the wind cooling them down on the warm summer day in the park.

Epilogue

Annie and Ian, side by side, held each other arm in arm, Annie, wearing a lovely lavender lace wedding gown, no poofy gowns for her, and Ian looking dapper in a white suit with a purple tie to accent his look, walking proudly down the park's path. They were all smiles as the wedding guests of all ages threw white rice over them, and they entered the hall.

Sitting among the guests at Palisades was Gayle, and her guy, Charles. They turned to look at each other, then at the bride and groom, as the little flower girls, Annie's nieces, tossed rose petals in the air while walking down the aisle behind the happy couple, and her little boy nephew, in a white suit who was the ring bearer shouted out his glorious exclamations while everyone cheered.

In the front row, Kay, wearing a light blue jacket with a rose bud complementing her silvery salt and pepper hair, and her husband Kenneth, sat smiling at their sons and daughters as they followed the couple and continued scattering the blossoms on Ian and Annie. Annie, from the corner of her eye, saw Mrs. and Mr. Chen clapping, their outfits graced with lily flowers in their buttonholes and suit pockets to honor the couple.

"Mommy, I think he is a much better match than the others," Ming Wen Chen smiled, his wife Nan Hua nodding in agreement. "I have something in common with the groom," he said, glancing sideways at his beautiful wife, then straight forward.

"Oh, what's that?" asked Mrs. Chen.

Turning to face her, he told her, "I chose the best mother of the bride ever!"

"Awwww, you always embarrass me, Ming Wen!" she said.

"Does this mean we'll renew our marriage vows?"

"It's been on my mind," rejoined Mrs. Chen, her smile shining bright.

"Will we do it right here, next month?" he asked, arms outstretched.

She nodded. "And that's how I like it!" said Nan Hua Chen, as she gave him a hug back, joining in the others' laughter on the cheerful summer day.

Acknowledgments

I'd like to thank my sister, who is always there to listen to my life challenges and to share the joys and the highs. Also, lots of love to my partner, who put up with my late nights working on this book.

Thanks to the people who inspired my characters for this book, Linda Bradshaw, Katherine Nielsen, Dappo Agorro, my childhood Chinese language schoolmates, including Vivian and Julie Tiao, Connie and Tonia Chao and their parents, and in memory of my nephew, who gave us joy. Thanks also to my niece, may you make your television writing dreams come true, and my brother-in-law for his good humor.

I can never thank my own dear parents enough. I know they are in a different life here, or waiting to join us soon again, near to us.

And thanks to Karen and Ed Adams, who allowed me to

envision what it would be like to have a wrap party in their home where they host Buddhist meetings for the sake of the happiness of our local members and friends.

Many thanks and memories with those aspiring screenwriters who shared insights, dreams and dialogue in the East Bay Screenwriters Group, even though it sometimes just functioned playing by ear and by the seat of our pants. You all inspired me to write more, whether it is a screenplay, children's book, or novel.

Thank you also to my readers who took a chance on taking in this debut novel of mine. I hope you will continue on when I write my upcoming works. And enjoy all of the fun. And to the romantic comedy and romance novel writers I have come to admire and be inspired by, I appreciate your art so much, whether in a book or onscreen. It brings me happiness and joy. Keep writing on!

Visit the author on the web:

www.geniechow.com

www.amazon.com/author/geniechow

www.facebook.com/geniemyo

www.instagram.com/artgal111

www.ingramcontent.com/pod-product-compliance
Lightning Source LLC
Chambersburg PA
CBHW020319200626
46814CB00006BA/2325